Born in the Grave Part 3

Lock Down Publications and Ca$h
Presents
BORN IN THE GRAVE 3
A Novel by *Self Made Tay*

Lock Down Publications
Po Box 944
Stockbridge, Ga 30281

Visit our website @
www.lockdownpublications.com

Copyright 2023 by Self Made Tay
Born in the Grave 3

First Edition February 2023
Printed in the United States of America

Lock Down Publications
Like our page on Facebook: Lock Down Publications
@
www.facebook.com/lockdownpublications.ldp
Book interior design by: **Shawn Walker**
Edited by: **Nuel Uyi**

Stay Connected with Us!

Text **LOCKDOWN** to 22828 to stay up-to-date with new releases, sneak peaks, contests and more…
Thank you.

Submission Guideline.

Submit the first three chapters of your completed manuscript to ldpsubmissions@gmail.com, subject line: Your book's title. The manuscript must be in a .doc file and sent as an attachment. Document should be in Times New Roman, double spaced and in size 12 font. Also, provide your synopsis and full contact information. If sending multiple submissions, they must each be in a separate email.

Have a story but no way to send it electronically? You can still submit to LDP/Ca$h Presents. Send in the first three chapters, written or typed, of your completed manuscript to:

LDP: Submissions Dept
Po Box 944
Stockbridge, Ga 30281

DO NOT send original manuscript. Must be a duplicate.

Provide your synopsis and a cover letter containing your full contact information.

Thanks for considering LDP and Ca$h Presents.

Chapter One

Flex

Grave Diggers

"Aaahhh!" I've never felt this pain before. Even when I attempted to kill Q myself, I never had to undergo this passive experience. After seeing his body fumbling to the ground, I screamed out in torture, feeling tormented to the core. The heartache shifted my mind into an intense state of unconscionable rage. If any motherfucker was gone take my brother's body from the soils of this earth and get away with it, it would be me.

With the draco held in my hands, I swiftly swung the aim in the direction of the Cadillac Escalade that was attempting to escape. Seems as though they were satisfied with dropping Q, who was their intended target. Sad to say, at least for them, they ain't have a clue who the fuck they were dealing with. I let off about a count of ten shots, aiming them all at the back tires of the spinning wheels, approximately splitting up five shots between the two. Air burst from both tires, causing the SUV to lose control. It swerved, missing the opening to exit the graveyard, slamming into the brick wall that surrounded the field full of tombstones. This time, vertically, I changed the purpose of my objective, making my target the back window of the now motionless vehicle. With evil aspirations, I sent scattering shots shattering the structure of the window, sending broken glass flying everywhere. Synchronizing my steps with my shots, I moved closer to the vehicle. With sharp shooting accuracy, I plucked a couple heads off. Them niggas must have been in a state of shock. No one but the passenger beside the driver attempted to return fire. I carved the nigga up like a turkey on Thanksgiving. The driver opened the car door and leaned his upper body out of the car, crawling to the ground.

I walked around the left side of the car and caught dude trying to climb to his feet. I ain't even want to kill him yet. I hit him in the shoulder as he whipped the gun off his waist. He dropped the pistol and fell back to the ground. I stepped up on him. Kicking the gun out of the reach of his arms, I placed the muzzle of the draco to the temple of his head and pressed it. "Who is you?" I asked through clenched teeth. "And why da fuck y'all niggas kill my brother?"

"Fuck you, pussy! I ain't tellin' you shit!" the already wounded man spat. "Suck my—" *Boc!* Can't say he ain't go out like a gangster. All them niggas was dead now. So, I really didn't care for the question I just asked. Think I already knew the answer anyway.

Snapping out of my state of rage, I took in everything that was going on around me. Q laid over to my left while Jay Jr laid off to the other side. My friends—or foes—Big Dee, Hawk, Blu, Red, and Wolf were still shooting for their lives, trying to kill of the handful of Richmond Police Department officers left over. For the longest time, I've been thinking that all this shit was my fault, making myself take all the blame. Now I was starting to reconsider. Maybe all of this really wasn't my fault. Maybe, just maybe, Q was the cause to this effect. He was the one that brung all of us together, tying us all in like the strings of a rope.

A forty-five-degree left turn of my body—and I focused on an officer occupied with ducking for his life. I gave his body a helping hand with finishing making its way to the ground, by sending three rapid shots, firing out the draco. One of the officers caught a whiff of his partner's falling body. How foolish of him to attempt to raise his gun at me. At this point, I was beyond the state of a super possessed maniac. Spitefully, I applied excessive pressure to the trigger of the rifle. The bullets ripped his body like a bear attacking the tent of a camper. About three more pigs now.

The attention of the coppers was mostly on me now. I gripped the baby chopper tighter in my grasp, preparing to do a clean sweep of the three little pigs that remained. However, all the draco gave me was clicks. Clip empty. Immediately, shots flew in my direction. I hurried my ass around to the other side of the crashed SUV and removed the Glock from my waist. I waited for the shots to let up so I could pop back up and return fire. They never did. They were smart. Or scared. There wasn't much of a distance between Q's laying body and I. I could easily shorten the distance with a sprint. Beside him laid the draco that he died with; I wanted to get to it.

Suddenly all shots came to a cease. *About time*, I thought to myself with my back to the Escalade. I was just starting to wonder what the fuck them other niggas were on.

I thought for sure they had left me for dead. To keep it a band with you, I was hesitant to poke my head out and take a peek. Wasn't too sure if them niggas would come for me next. Due to my survival, I realized that I had to look. When I did, I noticed that Hawk and Blu had took out one a piece, while Big Dee stood with a smoking gun over the same sucker cop who had took Jay Jr away from us.

Hawk looked over in my direction. Assuming that he would take aim, I hid back behind the truck. Still no shots. Instead, them niggas had ran down on me ninja style. So subtle that they caught the snake slipping. Me. With seven guns pointed in my face, Big Dee and Hawk had two, what was I to do? "Get yo' ass up, Flex!" Big Dee demanded.

"Let's smoke his ass!" Hawk suggested as I made my way off the ground.

"Naw," Big Dee disagreed.

"Wat?" Hawk asked, confused. "If we let dis snake ass nigga live, it's gone come back and bite us in da ass."

"No, it's not," Big Dee replied with assurance. "Cuz it's not gone come back."

"Huh?" The words slipped out of my mouth as I was now confused my damn self.

"You gotta go, Flex!" Big Dee ordered.

"Where da fuck I'ma go?"

"Ion kno' and Ion give a fuck. But you banded from da jets. And dis time if you even think 'bout poppin' up, I'll drop you myself. No hesitation."

"I'm tellin' you, Big Dee, dis is a bad decision." Hawk tried to intercede. "You kno' damn well dude ain't goin' fo' none of dat shit. If we let him walk away now, he just gone plot and lay on our asses 'til it's time fo' him to step again. Wat? You fo'got? Dis nigga is da reason dat most of our niggas are dead."

"I kno' dat, Hawk. I was der, remember? And da nigga did jus' help us out fo' once." I noticed Big Dee took a glance over at Q stretched out on the ground. "Besides, trust me—"

"I'll go." I think I took the words out Big Dee's mouth. "I promise I'll leave. Ion kno' where da fuck I'ma go. Dis all I kno', but I swear I'm gone. But only on one condition."

"Oh my God!" Hawk threw an arm up to the back of his head and scratched his scalp with the butt of the gun. "You don't have any room to bargain. Dis is not a fuckin' option. You either go, or you die."

I looked at Hawk with probably the dumbest face that I could express. I wanted to tell him that that was an option. Instead, I opted to my proposal. "Y'all niggas help me bury my brotha, brah, please? He would have done it fo' me." I mean literally dis nigga just had me digging my own grave just moments before all this shit happened. But I guess God had other plans. Guess that grave wasn't meant for me after all. Plus I had left my brother's body laid out in the streets once before. I couldn't live with doing it again.

"A'ight, man, we gone help da nigga," Blu mediated between Hawk and Big Dee. "But we gotta hurry up and do dis shit quick so we can get da fuck out of here. And you—" He flickered his gun at me. "After dis, yo' ass need to get gone like Simba."

We all walked over to Q's lifeless body. Tucking our pistols, all of us gave sharing hands in lifting Q, carrying him like pall barriers without a casket. Once we reached the dug-up grave, Big Dee looked up at me. "Drop him," I said. We tossed Q in the pit of the dirt. I picked up the only two shovels accessible in the graveyard and handed it to Wolf. "Help me out, lil' brah?" It was more like a request really. He grabbed it.

"Well," Hawk said, always sounding sarcastic, "guess y'all got it from here. Rest in peace, Q." The rest of the guys sent their blessings and said their goodbyes to Q. "Wat 'bout Jay Jr, though?"

"Leave him," Big Dee answered. "We'll get'em once da people done wit'em. Send him off da right way. Dis nigga Flex fucked up fo' dis shit." I was already throwing the dirt over Q's corpse. Hawk and the rest of the gang started walking off towards the graveyard wall that led to the projects. "Ayee." Everyone turned towards Big Dee who was still standing close to me. He tilted his head in the other direction. "Naw, under da bridge," he suggested. They all knew exactly what he was talking about, including me.

As Wolf and I continued to fill the hole in the ground with the earth's minerals, tears of sorrow flooded my eyes. Shedding tears had become suspended from my life since the funeral of my pops. Now I watched as a tear dripped from my eye into the soil that covered my brother's body. The more tears that fell, the angrier I became. I shifted the shovel with passion. It seemed that with every scoop then dump of dirt, a tear dropped to the ground. The dirt soaked up the liquid from my body, causing it to become moist. Soon I realized that I wasn't the only one crying. I looked up and noticed that dark clouds were circulating the graveyard, causing the heavens to pour down a sea full of tears of its own. The sound of thunder roared as lightning struck high above the sky. "Let's hurry up," I told Wolf. "Gotta get da fuck out of here."

Finally, the deed was done and I almost felt free to leave. Except there was just one thing. "You kno' wat?" I asked matter-of-factly as I threw the shovel off to the side.

"Wats up, brah?" Wolf asked. I ripped the gun off my waist and stuck it in his face.

"I was actually more loyal to you den my own fuckin' brotha. Wat fuckin' nerve do you have to betray me?" We stood in the midst of the pouring rain, getting drenched as the seconds ticked.

"I had to, brah! Dey was gone kill me." Now Wolf's eyes were filled up with tears. I knew that he knew he was already dead. Still, he pleaded. "Come on, brah! Please don't kill me. It's ova now. We made it out. We can—" *Boc!* I don't know what came over me so fast. Glad it did though. I ain't really have time for that soap opera shit.

"Cry me a fuckin' river." I removed the Glock from Wolf's waist and looked around for an escape route. Look like I'll be leaving this bitch on foot. "Damn!" I headed to the open gates of the graveyard. As I arrived to them, it was just my luck that a sounding set of sirens was headed up the street. I lifted both pistols but froze once the car closed in on me.

The car came to a halt and the driver door flew open. It was Lil' Shawty. I wasn't really sure what love was, but at that moment I think I had fell deeply into it. "Come on, boy!" She rushed to the back of the cop car. "Get yo' ass in da trunk."

"Oh my God, I think I fuckin' love you, Shawty, you—"

"Boy, shut up!" she said. "Get yo' ass in der." She pushed me into the back of the trunk and slammed it shut. Before I knew it, she was speeding away from the scene. I balled up in the trunk cold, wet, and uncertain of my future, yet thankful for this moment. And being thankful for me was something rare. Something new.

Self Made Tay

Chapter Two

Q

Battle of the Souls

Just when I thought life couldn't get any more complicated, the complications multiplied. After taking them shots to the head, I thought my works were done. Thought after I clocked out, it was time to rest up. To my surprise, the lights were only out for a few quick seconds. The first thing I saw, would have been hard for me to see with my physical eyes. The brightness could have blinded me, but it was easy for me to see past the glow. It was the Angel of Death. To my confusion, it was two of them. Neither of them resembled the depiction of our version of the Grim Reaper. Although one of them did carry that stick with the long sharp blade in his hand. He was made burning in a dark blue flame. Draped in a blue robe set ablaze. The other was made of pure light. Bright as the North Star. It was also covered in a robe. All white though. With illuminated white flames dancing amongst its garment. They both had two sets of wings on their backs. And they both moved in a perfect union while traveling closer to my laying body. The blue-flamed angel remarked: "Looks like this one is all yours. Seems as if he barely made the mark."

"Thank God they got him when they did," the Angel of Light replied. "He was just about to cross over to the other side. I don't like it when they let all those good deeds go to waste due to their pride. Watch out, I got this!" The angel struck its bare hands into my mouth and reached down my throat, reaching down to the bottom of my stomach at the base of my spine. Its hand got a hold of something. I don't know what it was, but it tickled when it made contact. The angel took a handful of whatever it was, and slowly pulled it up my spine. The feeling was one of the most pleasant feelings I've ever felt. The best way I could explain it to you was ecstasy. Talking about being high off life. While whatever it was rose up my spine, it felt as if the high was being elevated as it passed through the chakras of my body. Before I knew it, my soul was set free.

The first thing I did was look down at me. Well, I guess not me, but the body of my flesh. It laid there on the ground, the earth soaking up my blood as it spilled from my body. I no longer needed the blood to live. I was relieved from all the pains of my flesh.

"Hey, no need to cry over spilled blood. You won't be needing that body any longer. Heck, maybe you'll get another one," I heard the blue flame angel say. I looked up to the angels and realized that they were moving along, leaving me there to myself. I also noticed that they were big as—Wait a second. They were big as a—I couldn't curse. *What kind of sick twisted size are they!* I thought.

"Ayee!" I yelled out to the two tall angels that were almost triple my size. They only halfway turned to attend to me. "Where are you going? Don't you supposed to take me to heaven or hell or something?"

The two angels looked at each other as they paused. "Take him to heaven?" the blue flame angel asked the other. "Who he think he is? Jesus?" Both of the angels laughed out loud and continued on as they conversed. "What he got? A VIP ticket or something? Back stage pass? What he think this is? A concert?"

"You know I don't think they understand the basic instructions before leaving earth. Maybe it's just too complicated."

"Or maybe it's because they don't read it." Before I knew it, they both were disappearing into thin air literally.

"What the—" I mumbled to myself as I turned around. As soon as I did, a small cloud of smoke was poofing right before my eyes. Out of nowhere another angel appeared. She was beautiful and had a glow of light as well. Just a bit smaller than the last two angels. But still bigger than I was.

"Don't worry about them two. They just a couple of ass holes," the beautiful angel announced. "You can come with me."

"Huh?" was all my vocabulary allowed me to express.

"Yeah, fuck them. They boring anyway. We'll have lots of fun."

"But—I thought you were an angel?" It was astonishing to me that the angel could curse but I couldn't.

"I am an angel," she said, batting her eyes at me. "What? You don't think I'm pretty enough? Aren't you attracted to me?"

"I mean you are beautiful but—" Before I could complete my sentence, something shocking was knocking the pretty angel out of the sky, causing her to stagger to the ground harshly. I looked into the direction where the shock came from, only to find another angel floating in the mist of the air. She was even more beautiful and definitely bigger. She bared a harp in her hands that contained twelve strings.

"Stay down, Pig!" the bigger angel yelled out to the smaller one. Immediately, I wondered what would make one angel wound another. Suddenly I found out. The smaller angel disobeyed the command of the bigger one and rushed back into the air with rapid speed. She poofed into a cloud of smoke, causing me to think that she was gone. When the smoke cleared, I realized that the angel wasn't an angel. She was a pig.

"She is an angel," the bigger angel said. "She just a bad angel. Very evil and deceiving. And stop calling me that. My name is ZQ!" *Hold up. How does she know what I'm saying inside my head?*

"You don't have to talk to communicate here. Things work a lot different in the spiritual realm. Now get out of the way, quick! Go over and hide behind one of those tombstones!"

I did as I was told to do and ran. No, wait. Not *ran*. I didn't even have legs. I mean—well, I did, but it was as if they were merged together. Something similar to a merman minus the fin. My feet were almost totally gone. They resembled a swirling stream of smoke. So yeah, I floated. You know, like a ghost. You ever heard the saying be careful what you ask for? Prime example. Anyway, I made it to the far end of the grave-yard, to say the least, and got behind the tallest tombstone. From there I watched the battle take place. They were so big it was if I was still up close on them.

Pig was a unique looking pig. She still had the round snorkerly nose like Porky, but her ears were made like the horns of a ram. Pig covered her nose with one of her huffs and sneezed. The impact caused some green slimy stuff to roll out through her horns. "Excuse me," she said sarcastically while laughing. Barely missing ZQ, the green slime landed on the ground, burning up the grass as if it was acid. ZQ then played one single note of her harp by plucking a string. Another zap shot from the harp. It zipped to Pig in a zig zagging fashion and hit her, causing her to do her version of the Harlem Shake. Pig was relentless though, so back and forth they went.

Meanwhile I noticed that I had two different visions of reality, which led to me watching two different battles at once. Flex was releasing shots from the draco, aiming them at the vehicle that my murderer rode in. The truck crashed into the brick wall. Flex stepped towards it with determined steps. He shot one single shot. Then another. With that, the two Angels of Death returned. This time it was the blue flame angel's turn to snatch a soul. He swiped his sworded stick at the body of the man Flex had just killed. Instantly the tip of the sword was yanking the man's soul through his face. The soul screamed with so much terror it almost scared me. "Might as well stick around. Looks like Deshawn is on another rampage," said the blue flame angel, speaking of Flex while he moved on to yanking out the next soul.

"Yeah, and it looks like they are all dirty souls, yuck!" responded the white light angel. "I'm not touching them with my hands."

"Me neither. That's why I use this." As the blue flame angel referred to his soul-removing sword, he was just about to take another swing. Then he stopped. "Nope, looks like this one is yours. Another fence straddler."

With the more souls that the Angels of Death removed from the flesh of the bodies, I noticed the more demons or bad angels poofing up, trying to take them away. One demon popped up as dark as a shadow. "Aye, guys, it's a party going on up here!" he yelled to I don't know who, as he wrapped his arms around the soul of my murderer. "Got one," he said and then poofed. More demons showed up and I could see who the shadowy demon was talking to. All of them was itching for a soul to snatch. Through observation, I knew that the dark souls were easier to get a hold of, but the demons preferred the clean.

Flex continued on killing, now taking his rage out on the police. ZQ tried to save as many souls as she could but she was outnumbered a lot to one. Plus the dark souls went with ease, making it somewhat hard for her. Souls were floating around everywhere. Just as lost and confused as I am. ZQ took a stroke of her harp, almost pulling every string. The musical tone was a lovely sound but caused a wave to be released from the instrument. Something like a rock skipping across the lake. The wave reached all the demons present in the graveyard. It paralyzed them for a few seconds but they were able to shake back. I watched as two demons fought over the same soul, one knocking the other out with the harsh foul order of its breath. The demons were now filling the graveyard by the tens at a time, looking to claim the territory.

"Allah!" ZQ yelled out as she continued to zap demons. "A little help would be nice." As requested, help came. It was only one, though. He was as big as ZQ. There was a drum strapped to his back and a golden flute underneath his golden belt. It was so much going on that I almost missed my brother and the gang tossing my lifeless body back into the earth. Crazy thing to me is that, that was supposed to be Flex's grave. You plan, I plan, but Allah is the best of planners. The gang said their goodbyes and headed off.

I glided over to Flex and placed my hand on his right shoulder. "I love you, brah" was all I said. I knew that my words touched his heart because a tear fell from his eye. The angel with the drum pulled the drum around to his front side and pulled out two drum sticks. With a stick in each hand, he raised his right hand and brung it down on the drum with a loud boom. Then he used both sticks to set to set off a drumroll. It sounded like thunder. From a far distance a ladder was dropping from the sky. A handful of angels descended from the heavens. One angel appeared like a shooting star. He was much bigger than the rest. I watched as he tossed a lightning bolt further into the sky. The bolt struck a cloud. Out of the cloud dropped multiple lightning bolts striking the demons with electrical shocks. Most of the demons crumbled into piles of ashes. From there the other angels handled the rest.

"DeQuan, get out of the way!" the angel with the drum yelled out to me. "The name is Mark, by the way." Well, I listened to Mark and got back to my original spot. Demons were surrounded all around Flex. Mark tried to keep them from around him. One demon assisted Flex at lifting the gun to Wolf in the next moment he was being tempted to pull the trigger. Wolf's head cracked open from the bullet. Then his soul was being yanked out of his face. I revealed my face from behind the tombstone. Wolf looked around with a wicked smile at all the madness that was going on. That was until he saw me.

"Q! This shit all yo' fault!" He ran towards me as if he had intent to do harm.

"Nope," a demon said, snatching him by the neck. "Satan would be happy to see you. He's been waiting." He wrapped his arms around Wolf, then *poof*—be gone.

Flex ran off to I don't know where. All the demons were either ashes or had vanished away. After the Angels of Death snatched out Wolf's soul, they were gone. The other angels were now ascending back into the heavens. All except three. "ZQ, come with me. Satan is causing another ruckus in Chicago. Mark, take DeQuan to his grave please?"

"Yes, Archangel Michael," Mark said.

"And hey, Mark!" ZQ called out before heading off with who I now knew to be one of the most famous angels of all. "School the soul a little, please. It'll save us some warfare."

"Got you," the angel Mark said as the Archangel Michael and the angel ZQ zipped through the sky and disappeared like a UFO.

"What does he mean take me to my grave? My grave is right here, ain't it?" I questioned Mark.

"No. Your body will not remain here," he replied.

"How are you so sure of that?"

"Because Allah has revealed it to me. And through the mercy of him, I have the will to reveal it to you as well. Let me show you." Mark raised up both of his hands, touching them together above his head, making a triangle. He stretched his arms out in opposite directions as wide as he could and drew them down at its stopping point. I soon realized that he was drawing out a large screen. Like a projector. You know how the smart phones be, but on a much grander scale. He swiped right and tapped on what I guess was a video. He pressed *play* on the video and instantly we were in like another time zone. Same place though. It had to be a quick skip of about fifteen to twenty minutes later.

The scene was now filled with policemen, homicide detectives, forensics, and paramedics. Although it was no need for the last group of people. Everybody here was DOA. It took them a while to dig up the makeshift grave that Flex made. They even brung in a few more shovels to help speed up the process. Detective Graham and Detective Black, who were partners and leading Homicide Detectives in Richmond Virginia, stood side by side and waited for the evidence to unfold. "We got something here!" one of the grave diggers announced from about four feet in the grave. "It's looking like it's another body!" he shouted upward.

"What makes him so special?" Detective Graham asked his partner. "Guess we were a little late to the funeral. Hey, hey, take it easy from there. Don't want to cause any excessive damage!" Detective Graham yelled into the hole in the ground.

"Looks like a good thing if you ask me," Detective Black replied. "It's a massacre out here. Well over ten bodies."

"Did you take a look at any of the guys over there?"

"Naw, just the men we lost on the force and the Greene kid over there."

"Yeah, well, most of the guys over that way are unidentifiable. Signs say that they belong to some type of secret society."

Detective Black heard that and his face grew puzzled. "Who believes in crap like that?" he asked nonchalant.

"Same thing I said, partner. Same thing I said." The front of my body was partially revealed. Detective Graham anxiously jumped into the grave. He was in everything except a casket anyway.

"That's not nice," Mark said to me.

"Oh, my bad," I apologized. Forgot they could hear me.

Detective Graham bent down in the grave and with gloved hands dusted the dirt away from my forehead. "Well, I'll be damned." Detective Graham looked back up at his partner who was still standing at the top of the grave. "I guess the devil really isn't a liar after all. It's our favorite victim slash suspect. How the hell can anyone explain this?"

It's kind of a long story.

"Depending on which world you live in," Mark reminded me as he pulled the screen up again. Swipe, swipe, tap, and play. We were now at my funeral. It was kind of packed but the only people I paid any mind to was Keyshia and my two daughters who sat at the far right in the front row. And then Dawn and my newborn son who were just beneath me as I floated through the air alongside Mark. My son—Baby Q— looked up at me and that big smile of his spread across his face. If I ain't know any better, I could have sworn that he could see me. I floated left, his eyes followed. I floated right, his eyes followed still. "He can see us. Babies and little children are still spiritually connected to this realm. That's why they are so pure and innocent. By the age of seven this wicked world gets a hold of them, and the connection begins to fade," Mark informed me. With that being said, I made a funny face at Baby Q. He giggled, waving his arms, going crazy the way he like to do. He tried to match my funny faces with his, but all it caused him to do was blow out spit bubbles. Both Mark and I laughed at his attempt.

"Boy, wat is wrong with you?" Dawn asked our son as she wiped a single tear from her eye. "Why you actin' so silly?" I could tell the she was a bit embarrassed.

An elder lady leaned over the pew and whispered in Dawn's ear. Yet I was still able to hear her. "You kno' dey say dat some babies can spot an angel when dey come 'round."

Dawn stared down in our son's eyes for a few seconds before following his gaze, looking upwards. She placed a kiss in the open palm of her hand and blew it up towards me and uttered the words "I love you, Q." I caught the kiss and before I knew it, Mark was pulling up his screen again.

The next stop was Oak Wood Cemetery on Nine Mile Road. My casket was being lowered into the ground. Dirt was being thrown to fill the grave. Next thing I knew, I was in the grave. "I'll have to depart from you as of now. But who knows, we might meet again, Insha Allah."

"Huh? wait. So you mean I have to stay here? For how long? When will I get my angel wings?"

"You are a soul. Not an angel. Why would you want to be an angel? We technically work for souls as part of our worship to Allah. And I don't know how long you would have to stay here. It all depends on the mercy that Allah gives you and your soul's status."

"So, you can't find out my—" He was gone. I was left alone again. In the dark.

Chapter Three

Flex

In Too Deep

The brakes squeaked and the car came to a stop. I heard a garage door closing down, and the car door opening. The trunk of the car popped open, and I hopped out shivering cold. Lil' Shawty met me coming around the back end of the car. I was about to give shawty a big ass hug. If you knew me, even a least bit, you would know how much I hated hugs. But this bitch, with her brave ass, had the nerve to smack the shit out of me. Bitch must have forgot that I was a gangster. "Dats cuz you so fuckin' hard-headed!" She scowled at me. "I told yo' ass to pipe down some. We were 'posed to focus on da money, Flex. You and yo' stupid ass ego." She was right. I did it again. Fucked everything up. Looks like this fuck up was the final one. I can't even see myself making it out this one. I probably was better off burying myself alive with my brother's corpse.

"Umm—I understand da love connection y'all got goin' on. It's cute and all dat but we need to get rid of all dis evidence befo' all dis shit really come crashin' down on our heads." That was Two. Just in case you was late to this psycho saga of mine, I got a few dirty cops working on the other side of the field with me. Well, I wouldn't really call them dirty. So let's just say *fed up*, to sum it up.

"You right, Two," Lil' Shawty said, shifting her attention from me to Two. "But we also need a place to go. We can't stay in dis fuckin' city." Out of all this shit they was talking, the only word I was actually hearing was 'we'. What the fuck do they mean *we*?

"Hold up, wat da fuck do y'all mean *we?*" I just had to ask.

Both Lil' Shawty and Two looked at me dumbfounded. "Nigga, wat da fuck do you mean, *Wat da fuck do y'all mean we?*" she emphasized. "We made a pact with you in da beginning to ride dis shit all da way out til' da end. As far as I'm concerned, we still breathin' so dis shit ain't ova." I looked over towards Two.

"Wat?" she asked, still popping her bubble gum the way she always did. "Fuck dis police shit. It's time to take dis show on da road." I smiled my famous smile which you may mistake as an evil grin, feeling like a proud father watching his kids graduate. I looked in between the two of their heads and set my sights at the back of One. He was sitting in his usual spot behind the desk.

"I think I found a place," one said, staring at the computer screen. "We could at least go der 'til we figure da next move out." Hold up, hold up, hold up it was starting to be to many we's. I was gone have to tell somebody no. "Looks like you got family out der," one said, now spinning one hundred and eighty degrees in the chair. Family? I don't have any family. Only family I know of is my nieces by Q.

"Wat do you mean by *family?*" I questioned One, casting a glance between the two women as I headed towards the computer.

"Brothas. Two of them. Twins. In south Boston, Virginia."

"Dat can't be true. How did you find dat out?"

"Come on, Flex, have I let you down thus far? I was lookin' through yo' father's criminal history and saw a domestic dispute on a Cindy Yolanda Jones."

"Cindy Yolanda Jones?" I mumbled.

"Yeah, I looked her up. She was convicted of possession of weed way back in da day. At da time she lost two sons to the system. A De'Mon and a De'Angelo Anderson. Coincidence? I think not. Pull up pics." He clicked the mouse once. "To say dey favor you would be an understatement. Yo' Pops must have had some real strong genes. And when it comes to criminal history, I don't kno' who is worse, you or him."

"How da fuck was you able to find all dis out?"

"I jus' told you. Wat part did you miss?"

"No, wat I really meant was dat if you can find dis shit den I'm pretty sure dey can too."

"Yes, unless—" He was typing away at the keyboard. "Transfer data." Some more typing. "And den delete. Out of da system!" he said and removed a USB card from the computer. "And onto here. Jus' in case we need it." *Boc!* Yes, I killed the nigga. Shot his ass right in the head. Point blank range. He used the word *we* one to many times.

"Flex, wat da fuck is wrong wit you?" Lil' Shawty snapped at me while smacking me in the back of my head. "We could have used him."

"Fo' wat?" I asked. "Dis ain't no 007 mission. It's simply *get da fuck out of dodge*. Everything dat we needed from him is right here on dis USB." I had the card in my hand, placing it in my pocket.

"Dats yo' fuckin' problem. You think you too smart fo' yo' own good." You know what's crazy? I said that very same thing about Q. "And yo' ass don't have no fuckin' loyalty."

"I do have loyalty," I said in my own defense.

"Oh yeah? Well, to who, Flex?"

"To me!" I said through clenched teeth as I yoked the bitch up by the throat, bringing her to her tippy toes. "And listen here, you lil' bitch you. Yo' ass better apply dat same loyalty to me as well. you kno' wat? I thought I was fallin' in love wit yo' ass. And maybe I am. But even love ain't enough to stop me from killin' yo' dumb ass. Oh yeah, and let me tell yo' ass one more thing—"

"I can't—breath. Flex." She had both of her hands wrapped around my wrist, but it wasn't enough to stop me from applying pressure.

"Flex, let her go, please!?" Two sounded like she was about to start crying. But at least the bitch stayed in line.

"If you eva put yo' hands on me again outside of sex, I jus' might give yo' ass wat you lookin' fo'. Do I make myself clear?"

"Yes," she replied in a raspy choking voice. I released my grip, allowing her to gasp for air. What happened next, though, was very much to my surprise.

Lil' Shawty detached the pistol from her holster in cowboy record speed and aimed the gun at my head from a distance. Swift and smart. I thought to myself. "OK, now it's my turn," she stated with more confidence than I've ever seen before in her. "Da way I see it, you stuck in dis pile of shit jus' as deep as we are. Da tables are turnin' now so I strongly suggest dat dis shit goes both ways. Matter of fact, dats a high demand. Now, if you'll stop thinkin' wit yo' dick head and *think*, you'll realize dat we have da body of a cop layin' here. And dat da wise thing to do would be to get da fuck out of here, now!"

"A'ight, Lil' Shawty, you got it. You got it!" I said, actually honest, with both of my hands up. "But you gangsta though. I knew I loved you. My lil' bitch psycho. Bitch gotta be crazy comin' at me like dat."

"Flex, seriously, get yo' ass in da trunk so we can get da fuck out of here!" By now she had put her gun back into its holster.

"A'ight, I got you." I was making my way back to the already open trunk. "But I'm sayin', though, you don't wanna ride back here wit me? We can find a way to make a fuck scene. You got a nigga horny as shit right now."

Both Lil' Shawty and Two pushed me inside the trunk. "Boy, shut da fuck up!" they said in unison.

"Damn! I ain't kno' dat nigga talked dis much," said Two. They closed the trunk together and hopped in the car.

Chapter Four

Q

Back in the Grave

Sitting in the silenced darkness, I searched for a sight but saw nothing. I listened for a sound, but heard nothing. While doing nothing, I tried to contemplate how everything or anything all come from nothingness. Thought I was on to something. Thought something had come to me like the bright idea of the invention of the light bulb. Before I could figure out what was going on, my whole grave was lit up with light. After about— I don't know how long, I could see again. It was another angel. I came to realize that all the angels I've seen so far, good or bad, were all created of some type of flaming fire. Smokeless. This angel was bigger than the usual ones I'd seen as well. About the same size as The Archangel Michael.

"Yes, my name is Gabriel. I am also considered an Archangel. I am the chief messenger angel of Allah." He sat in front of me with his legs crossed Indian style. From the light of his flames, I was able to actually see inside the grave. The best way I could understand was, imagine the dirt that filled the grave was never there. Except the top layer where the grass grew. "I am here to ask you the questions of the grave that all souls are asked."

"Okay," was all I replied.

"Who did you worship as your Lord?"

"Allah," I answered truthfully. Well, at least to the best of my abilities.

"What religion did you practice?"

"Islam."

"Who was the messenger?"

"Prophet Muhammad. Peace and blessings be upon him."
With my last answer, the dirt walls of my grave began to
widen and at the same time brighten itself out its darkness.

"You have been rewarded with a spacious grave for your
worship and good deeds. You will not have to wait in darkness
any longer."

"But what am I waiting for?" I was curious.

"For your body to fully return to the earth through its de-
composing process. And although you are still a soul with a
free will, until your body is totally a part of its original sub-
stance, you will have to remain at your grave. At least until
further command from our Lord. However, Allah has sent me
with a mercy to bless you with any visit of your choice."

"Only one?" I asked ignorantly.

"Only one," the angel replied with assurance. "And it
would be wise to show a little gratitude for that one, for it is
truly a miracle."

"Sorry, may Allah forgive me for my ungratefulness."

"Allah forgives all who repents sincerely. Now whom
would you like to visit?"

"My daughters," I replied without hesitation. Other than
my own funeral it's been some time now since I've seen them.
Too much time. As a matter of fact, the last time was when I
was running out of their lives and ran into death. The Archangel Gabriel drew up his screen exactly how Mark had done.
Literally, in no time we were in the room of my two daughters.

"Your time is unlimited for the visit. Though I must warn
you that they can see you and as long as no other eyes draw
within your sight, the visit will last. The only grounds of ter-
minations are exposure." I heard what Gabriel was saying and
I was listening as well. However, I was already drawing near
to De'Mia who stared up at me with wide eyes.

"Daddy!" De'Mia yelled out in joy. She dropped the doll babies and hurried towards me. We met. She tried to give me a hug, but ended up wrapping her arms around herself. I was able to hold her in my embrace, though.

"Where?" De'Asia asked, turning away from the TV in disbelief. Once she saw me, she ran over to her sister and I. They hugged each other. "Daddy, why you leave us? We was lookin' fo' you all dis time," she said.

"Yeah, Daddy, and why Mommy said you weren't comin' back?" De'Mia questioned. "And we seen you in dat bed at church fakin' like you was sleep."

"Yeah, and we tried to wake you up. But you got us good dat time. Big head still play too much." De'Asia swung at my head but only harmed the air.

"And you had everybody cryin' too, Daddy."

"I kno' right. Mommy was real sad. I kept askin' her why she was cryin.'"

"Dats when she said you weren't comin' back, and we thought dey put you in da ground." De'Mia turned sad as if she was reliving the day of my funeral, then she went on, "But I was like unh unh. I was gone jump in der and get my Daddy." She suddenly burst with full energy. I had to laugh.

"OK, listen. I need to tell y'all something." I swear when it came to these two, you knew everything about the creation of God without having to utter a word throughout the conversation. "First of all, Daddy loves y'all more than anything in this world. And I'm only here right now as a visit. And I don't know but God willing I'll be able to come back and visit you two every chance I get. Or who knows, maybe even better we'll be able to be together again completely."

"So wat Momma said was true? Wat we saw was real?" asked De'Asia.

"Yes, De'Asia." I had to look into her watered eyes as I broke her heart with the truth. "I would never play a mean game on you like that. But hey, hey, look at me." She was starting to lower her gaze, dropping her head to the ground. "As long as it's up to you two, I'll always be with you right here and right here." I used both of my hands to point to the both of their hearts and their brains. "We will always be connected. I am running all through your DNA. Never forget that and please promise me one thing." They looked on with attention. "Always put God first."

"OK," they said in unison, both nodding.

"But Daddy do you have to go now?" De'Mia wanted to know.

"No. Not at this moment."

"So can we play fo' a while?"

"Sure we can."

"Yayyy!" They jumped up in joy. "Tag, you it!" De'Asia tried to start a game of Tag before sucking her teeth in disappointment. "You cheatin', Dad. You see through like a ghost." I laughed again. Couldn't help it.

"Probably can't play Tag, but we can definitely play Tickle Monster!" I grabbed both of them by the bellies and tickled them furiously, causing them to buckle down at the knees, stumbling to the floor. They laughed hysterically, crying tears of joy. De'Mia just about couldn't take it anymore. She reached for the doll baby that she played with earlier and tossed it at my head. Of course, it flew through the wind, slamming into the wall.

"De'Asia, De'Mia, y'all asses better not be in der fightin' again!" I heard Keyshia's voice approaching the closed door to their room. She swung the door open and rushed in only to see them rolling on the floor in laughter. "Wat da hell is y'all crazy ass gurls doin' now?"

"We playin' Tickle Monster wit Daddy," De'Mia replied.

Keyshia sucked her teeth in disbelief. "Gurl, yo' Daddy is not in here. I told y'all already dat—"

"Unh Unh, Ma." De'Asia cut her mother off in mid-sentence. "He right—" She was pointing towards me but could no longer see me. "He was jus' right here."

De'Mia pouted. "Mommy made him disappear. She always runnin' Daddy away."

"No. Don't say dat. Yo' Daddy was grown and he made his own choices in life." Keyshia bent down to be on an eye-to-eye level with the girls. "But like I said, he is not—"

"Nope, Mommy!" De'Asia cut her off again. "Don't say dat again because Daddy never left. He right here." She pointed to her mother's heart. "And right here." Then her brain.

"Yep, she right, Mommy!" De'Mia vouched. "Dats wat Daddy jus' said." Keyshia hugged our two princesses tight and held them as she looked up in to the sky. A tear rolled down her eyes, but I think it was a tear of relief.

As quick as one could snap their fingers, it was back to the mud for me. At least I had space to do nothing. And light to see nothing. But hey—who am I to be ungrateful for anything, right? I peeped into my casket and saw that my body was still intact. This may take a while. With nothing to else to do, I laid back on top of the casket and rested my soul in peace.

Chapter Five

Flex

Mania in a Resting Place

I let the heated water from the shower head pour over my head and drip down my body. Thoughts of the past year flashed through my mind at lightning speed. It was that bad. All the bodies lost. All the hate that exposed the fake love. Time wasted. All for nothing. Realizing now that I was a man truly blinded, I was full of regrets. Never thought that these feelings would run through me. Looking back at it now, I wish I would have done better.

"How are you so sure dat we can trust him?" I heard Two's voice in the hotel bedroom as I turned the water off.

"Jus' believe me, Two," Lil Shawty replied. "Everything will be alright. We need him and as long as we remain valuable to him, he'll be able to use us fo' some. Keep us wit him. Besides, wat else we gone do? Turn ourselves in to da jail? We're jus' as responsible fo' dis shit as he is. And I'm pretty sure da cops are lookin' fo' us as well. Ders no way we can turn around now."

After I finished drying my body off, I wiped the dew away from my face and starred into the fogged mirror. I only saw the figure of myself through a cloud of steam. I didn't even think about wiping the mirror clear. Didn't want to see my true self. The man that I've become was basically dead. A soul destined for hell. With nothing but a towel wrapped around my waist, I exited the bathroom of the hotel. I walked into the double-bedded hotel room, then both Lil' Shawty and Two froze in awe at my half naked body. "Wat?" I asked, acting as if I was lost. "Y'all actin' like y'all never saw a naked man befo'.'" I flopped down on the bed nearest to me and grabbed the remote to the TV. One hand resting behind my head, one leg stretched out on the bed, and the other still connected to the floor, I purposely showed off. Although I was living like a demon, my body was chiseled like one of those fake ass god statues. I had even lost a little weight but all it did was make my muscles stick out even more.

"Gurrll," Two said, stretching the word out.

"He gets on my last nerve," Lil' Shawty confessed.

"I see why though. Shidd! He can get on mine too." I looked over to the two beautiful dime pieces who seemed sexier as ever while they counted up stacks of money. Lil' Shawty was looking over at Two, like, *As if you really want him to get on yours here and now*. I caught Two locked in on the snake print resting under the towel. She noticed me watching her check me out and tried to look away and get back to what she was doing.

"Wat?" Two asked defensively, setting her sights on Lil' Shawty. "Shidd—We sharin' da consequences. Mattas well share da pleasures too."

"Wateva." Lil' Shawty partially rolled her eyes. "Stay focused. How much you got so far?"

"Fifty-five." The look on Lil' Shawty's face said it all. "Wat?" Two still on the defense. "A bitch was shoppin'. You kno' I ain't never had shit. Everybody ain't spoon fed like you, hoe."

"Boo-hoo." Lil' Shawty let out a fake cry. "Anyway, dis one fifty right here so far. So we still at a good pace." I wasn't gone say nothing but the conversation I overheard Lil' Shawty and Two having was all wrong. Shit, I needed these bitches so bad that my life depended on it. I don't know what I've would have done if Lil' Shawty had not come pick me up out the middle of the street. I ain't have shit. Not even a place to go. I was so relieved that I had them by my side to share my pains with and lighten the fall. Guess I did something right by placing them where they at because now it was all coming back to me. I was paying them off bi-weekly with ten bands apiece in an envelope. So when Lil' Shawty said one-fifty, I assumed and hoped she meant thousands of course. "Flex, wat you got, Boo? It's best if we budget it all together."

I was slow to respond, acting as if I was fully focused on the TV and paying no mind to what they were doing. Still playing into my I-don't-need-a-bitch cocky role. But I couldn't lie if I wanted to. "I ain't got shit." Once again, this time with my words, I froze them.

"Wat?" they questioned together as if it was planned. "Wat you mean you ain't got shit?" Lil' Shawty felt the need to take charge of the interrogation.

I think I spent a little bit of too much time around Lil' Shawty. I was definitely starting to rub off on her. I looked over towards her with my evil eye. "Wat part of 'I don't have shit' don't you understand?"

"But how not?" She wasn't fazed. It kind of amused me and pissed me off at the same time. "I watched you. We watched you and helped you make all dat money."

"Listen, bitch." I felt forced to get up from my comfort spot. Standing in front of the night stand, I damn near ripped the drawer out of it. "Dis is all I got." I pulled out one Glock .40. "And dis." I pulled out another one. Reaching down to the floor, I snatched up my jeans that laid there. Digging into the pockets of my Amiri's, I pulled out a wad of bills. I flung the pocket change that accumulated up to about fifteen hundred across the room to the other side of the bed. Most of the bills detached from each other, falling loosely from the sky like drops of rain. "Da rest of da cash I got is back at my stash spot 'round da projects." Feeling deflated, I sat back on the bed with my back to them.

"Let's go get it," Two suggested clearly not thinking.

"Hell naw!" Lil' Shawty and I matched tones.

"Dat shit ain't even worth killin' fo'," I said, now laying back on the bed. "Besides," I added, "dem niggas probably already got dey hands on it by now. Let dem niggas have it. Dey deserve it." Looking up at the ceiling, I felt like a failure all over again. I was wrapped up in my arrogance, my greed, and my pride that I can't even recall where I went wrong. Or maybe my whole foundation was rocky from the start. But I thought I was clever. Thought I had it all figured out. But if that wasn't the formula, then my whole way of whipping up a plan was disastrous. It felt like torture trying to make myself sit through this slump enduring the pain with patience. I never had patience. Whenever I felt this way I'll spin like the Tasmania Devil, causing havoc to any and everything in my way. Selfishly sabotaging anything anybody had that was special to them to sooth my own anxiety. Just the fact that I was admitting this denounced delusion provided hope at the end of the tunnel. That's if I make it to the end. For I was sure that the trip would be a long, lonely, and timely travel.

"It's cool anyway," Lil' Shawty said, bringing me out of my miserable mind. This reminded me that I wasn't completely alone, yet. "We got a lil' ova two hundred thousand right here. It'll hold us well off 'til we figure out something permanently." *Damn*, I thought to myself. *Yeah, it's stamped.* I knew I loved that bitch. Coming to that conclusion revealed a new regret of mine. Wish I would have taken her more serious from the get-go. I think the fact that she was law enforcement made it hard to trust her. But then again, I ain't trust no bitch, or anybody for that matter. Maybe I should try now, especially when my choices are so slim. Got me going out on a limb.

"Wats wrong, Flex? You not actin' like yo'self." Two's voice showed concern for my unusual base level energy.

"Yeah, I'm good," I said, faking. Acting as if I was tuned into the television.

"Why you always got to pretend to be so damn gangsta?" Lil' Shawty picked up on my act.

"I ain't pretendin'. I'm coolin'."

"Boy, wateva, dat pride gone be da death of you if you don't kill it first. While you ova der actin' like you all up in da TV. Probably don't even kno' wat da hell you watchin'. Wat da fuck is dat anyway?"

"History channel. Ancient Aliens."

Two busted out in laughter, damn near spitting her teeth out her mouth. "Ancient wat? You believe in dat shit?" She giggled out.

"Some of des theories be true though," I responded in my defense. "Dey talk 'bout aliens in da Bible and everything. Dis episode talkin' 'bout da book of Enoch right now."

"Gurl, dat probably explains why da nigga so fuckin' crazy!" Lil' Shawty emphasized. "He probably was abducted by one of dem. Dey changed his DNA or some experimental shit like dat." They shared a laugh. Glad they were in a good mood. Luckily for them, I was trying my best to refrain from being me. Otherwise, I'd find a way to make them carry the burdens of my sorrows while making myself merry off making them the miserable one.

"Oh naw, gurl, dis may be serious. His ass ain't talkin' shit or none."

"Told you," Two agreed.

"Flex!" Lil' Shawty called out to me in a motherly tone.

"Yo."

"Are you sure you OK?"

"Yee." But I swear if one of them ask me that shit one more time—

"You hungry? You want some food or some?"

"Ion think we should leave dis room 'til it's time to hit da road fo' good." What I really wanted was drugs. "Y'all already stopped enough as it is on the way here." They stopped once to switch up the car, and twice to pick up their monies and other shit that I paid no mind to.

"We don't have to leave. Dis five stars, baby. It's called room service."

"A'ight," I simply said, not thinking, just trying to cut the conversation short.

Lil' Shawty walked over and sat beside me on the bed where I laid. "Scoot ova, punk!" she demanded, playfully nudging me in my rib. "Listen." She gently placed a hand on my bare chest. "I kno' you jus' lost yo' brotha and you probably have a lot goin' through yo' mind right now. Honestly, I can't say dat I understand but I do emphasize. Regardless of how you feelin' or da motions dat you're goin' through I want you to always keep in mind dat I am here fo' you."

"We." Two cut her off by clearing her throat.

"Right, *we*," Lil' Shawty corrected, "are here wit you, fo' you, and we gone ride dis bitch 'til da wheels fall off. Do you hear me?"

It took a few seconds for the words to sink in. But when they did, the meaning melted my heart like acid touching rubber. I was getting soft and fast. I was more vulnerable than I've ever been. Had me wondering what I did to deserve this type of love. All I knew was that attitude towards life was changing. Instead of taking things for granted, I was becoming grateful. "Yeah, I hear you, Lil' Shawty." I tried my best to be nonchalant. "We gone see."

"You right 'bout dat. But first," she said, getting all jolly and shit, bouncing around, trying her best to be ghetto. Reminded me of Nu-Nu of ATL. I wasn't mad though. It was cute. I knew the bitch was faking. "We gone order us some food, relax, and clear our minds befo' it's time to hit dis road. Wat you wan' to eat?" She picked up the phone off the night stand.

Cocaine, I said in my mind. I was way too down right now. Needed my upper. "Shidd, it don't even matta fo' real. You pick," I then verbalized.

Lil' Shawty ordered the food for Two, herself, and I. Switching channels, I turned on Starz on-demand and caught up on dat new BMF show. As if I wasn't already feeling bad enough, shit made me think about Q punk ass even more. I ain't realize it until now but Q was my heart. Now that he was gone, I felt that for sure a piece of me was definitely missing. Also, I noticed that he was actually smarter than what I initially gave him credit for. Smart enough to cheat death. And smart enough to lay low long enough to plot a plan of revenge. Clever motherfucker almost had me. Caught me sitting like a duck. I wonder if he was really gone kill me. Like really try to do me the way I tried to do him? I couldn't put my finger on exactly what it was, but something about life had changed Q. I mean if your brother tried to kill you, I'm pretty sure it would change you too. But it seemed like a little something more than that. Something demonic, satanic.

Going into my memory bank, something had hit me like a robber at the teller. The Rolls Royce. The bitch. The last time I'd seen it and sprayed it up. Only to find Reggie in the driver's seat. The passenger that hopped out and ran. The hunch I felt when he sent shots back at me. I was enlightened now that not only once, but twice in my lifetime I had gunned for my brother. Damn. So he was there the whole time. I wondered for how long, though. What else was he doing right under my nose that I was so blind too? How the fuck did he get that Rolls Royce?

"Damn!" Lil' Shawty and Two collaborated on an expression. "See, now dats fucked up." Two went solo. Big Meech had finally clipped Lamar like a grey hair. Afterwards, his right hand smoked his own girlfriend whom he actually was in love with. Both of the ladies were looking over at me in shock, searching for reaction.

"Bitch was disloyal," I simply said, putting my attention on the TV show that I was only half watching at the time.

Two sucked her teeth as if she was unpleased with my answer. "Bitch was disloyal though," Lil' Shawty agreed. "But still, maybe it was a lesson fo' her to learn in all dat. Dey could have at least gave da bitch time to redeem herself." Do disloyal people deserve second chances? I was only asking myself. Then I thought, hell no! Only a fool would take that risk.

There was a knock at the door. "Room service."

"Bout damn time," Lil' Shawty said, urgently swaying her way to the door. I grabbed one of the Glocks that were still stretched out on the bed, and rested it under my right thigh. The other, I slid underneath the pillow. Call me crazy. Call me paranoid. Insane. Overdramatic. Or whatever else you could think of. But the way my mind has been roaming, I wasn't trusting shit. Zip. Not a goddamn thing. Lil' Shawty popped the door open and allowed room for the man in a black and white suit step into the room with a cart full of food. Everything seemed normal, so I guess there was no need to panic. Guess it was due to all the wrong I had done that made something just not feel right. Felt like the world was out to get me.

Maybe even you. Off a pure habitual instinct, I laid my right hand under my thigh and lightly fondled the handle.

"Good evening," was all the man said as he started to move some things around on the cart. I was ready to shoot. He seemed nervous and a bit unsure with his actions. Besides, he could have done all that shit before he brung his ass up here. Given the benefit of doubt, maybe he was new to the job. A rookie. I observed him as he glanced up to observe the room. Another sign. I'm pretty sure that if you worked for room service at a hotel you knew what the rooms looked like by now. Unless he was trying to check my bitch out. The second one, Two. Lil' Shawty was back at the bedside next to me. There were two main course meals on top of the cart. Both sat under a silver rounded top that concealed the heat of the food inside. The room waiter grabbed for the one closest to him. Then he hesitated cutting his eyes up at me while looking down. Yeah, he a rookie, I thought to myself. But not in the fashion that I was speaking on before.

I shoved Lil' Shawty off the bed from her sitting position, pushing her to the floor. Simultaneously, I unconcealed the Glock from under my thigh, swinging it around to take aim. The room service guy was hip by now. Although he was late by the calculation of time, he still tried. Flipping the top of the tray that held no food, he reached for the gun. It was fun while it lasted. *Boc! Boc!* I let off two shots, sending them both to his head. "Wat da fuck!" Lil' Shawty screamed in confusion.

I noticed something moving underneath the curtains of the serving cart. "Get down, get down!" I ordered as I was rolling over to the bed. Immediately, I hit the floor. Soon after, shots were sailing through the wind. The sound effects of the shots were abnormal. Almost like a quiet whistle. Like spit balls. My first instinct was to look under the bed to get a shot at the gun man's feet. I couldn't hit. Lil' Shawty had hid under there. Military style, I crawled to the foot of the bed, trying to get a better view. Bullets skipped on the floor in front of my face, damn near missing my nose by an inch. Shit was so close I damn near felt the heat from the speed of the bullet. I backed the fuck up. Started to panic. Had every reason too. Nigga had me pinned to the floor. I anticipated for the second shooter to come over top of the bed. Instead, I heard slow steps approaching going around the bed. I had to make a move and now before we all ended up dead in this bitch. This movie would be over before it even got started. Plus I wasn't ready to face God yet. I had some cleaning up to do first. *Bocca! Bocca! Bocca! Bocca!* "Wat da fuck!" I had flinched from the sound of a third gun being fired off. Mainly because I was curious as to where the hell they came from.

A body collapsed in the area where the footsteps where just stepping only moments ago. "Ughhhhh!" The sound of someone throwing up came from the other side of the bed. I knew that it could only be one person. Two.

Climbing to my feet, I rushed over to the second shooter to make sure he was dead. The nigga was a midget. Baby Go Go Gadget ass nigga had two guns with silencers screwed to them. I took them both. From further examination I noticed that he had a ring on his pinky finger. Thinking back, it was the same ring that my Pops use to wear. I know because I admired it so much. Always used to try to figure out what that symbol stood for.

"You OK, Two?" Lil' Shawty asked, coming from under the bed, holding her stomach. Two just nodded.

"First time killer," I assumed, looking at Two. She nodded some more. "You did dat shit like a pro. Stomach a lil' weak though."

"Fuck you," she managed to grumble.

"Wat da fuck is dis?" Lil' Shawty asked, surprised.

"It's a crime scene. And we don't want to be here when yo' people pull up. We need to go, now!"

"But how did you kno'?"

"I'm da muscle, baby. A hitta. Dats how I knew!" I said with the same foolish pride that got me this far in life. "Now, let's go!" Lil' Shawty was looking at me as if I was a fool or something. I couldn't understand why until she looked down to my muscle hanging freely. The towel had fallen from my waist a long time ago. I was completely naked.

While I threw on my clothes, Lil' Shawty and Two packed the little things that we did have. Two suitcases was too much baggage, if you ask me. But I understood that one was filled with money. Before exiting the room, Lil' Shawty handed me a Boston Red Sox New Era fitted cap and a pair of Versace frames. The old joints like Biggie used to wear. "Wat da fuck?" I asked, almost under my breath.

"Boy, put da shits on." I snugged the fitted cap over my head, and she rested the frames on the bridge of my nose.

"You 'possed to want me to blend in. Not stand out. Don't nobody wear des shits no more." As I walked past the first shooter laying on his back, I noticed that he had that same exact ring on. I logged it into my mental and kept moving.

Lil' Shawty was the first one out the door. She moved as if there wasn't just a shootout behind those closed doors. I followed behind her with a grip on one of Two's hands, pulling her along as she dragged the suitcase on its wheels. Of course, there were a few people poking their heads out the door but as we passed by, they grew fearful and took they nosey asses back in their rooms. Probably to call the police. "Is everything alright down there?" an elderly white woman asked as we approached the elevator.

"Oh no, ma'am," Lil' Shawty assured. "Everything is fine. My firearm had jus' accidently discharged. I'ma police officer." She flashed her badge at the old woman.

"Oh, good then. I thought something terrible had happened."

"Nope, everything is fine like I said." I was happy as fuck when that elevator door opened. I ain't want to have to kill this old lady. But something in me was just itching to do it. We stepped onto the elevator. As the doors closed, the old lady stood there staring at us with a questionable look upon her face. Two floors down the elevator stopped again. We were on the fifth floor. A black suited man stepped onto the elevator with us. He saw that his desired destination was already chosen on the elevator panel and simply stood in front of us as the doors were concealing again. He cleared his throat and adjusted his tie. I clutched. He turned halfway over his shoulder, taking a peek before returning his head back in its forward position. As quietly as possible, I drew one of the pistols that I got from the shooter I left slumped back in the room from my waist. Second floor. First floor. Garage. *Pssh! Ding!* As soon as I dropped him, the elevator doors were retracting. Lil' Shawty looked at me with a half disgusted look on her face.

"Wat?" I was nonchalant as hell. "He looked suspect."

"Yo' ass must wanna go to jail," she said, stepping over the fresh corpse lying at the floor of the elevator.

"Hell naw." My reply was defensive as if I hadn't committed a crime ever in my life. "I ain't tryna die either though."

"Let's get da fuck out of here, please?" We found the car and swiftly made our way to the parking deck exit.

Chapter Six

Q

Back in the Field

In the midst of my peaceful rest, which was far from a sleep, but more like a meditation, I was disturbed by the sounds of repeated knocks. I opened my eyes and looked around. No one was there. Getting off the casket I was laying on, I took a peek inside. There, my physical body still laid stiff as a log. I closed the top to the casket and heard the knocks again. Quickly I opened the casket again and pondered at the corpse strangely. I was starting to think that the physical form of myself was playing a cruel trick on me. I smacked it in the face twice to see if it would move. Nothing. Still as reposed as the Statue of Liberty. Almost thought I'd seen it crack a smile. But it was all in my conscience. The knocks came again. This time I was sure it wasn't the corpse. I was looking right at me. "Q!" I heard a voice call. "You in there?" A very familiar voice at that. "Pop out."

"Pop out," I said to myself in a wondering voice. I looked around for a way out. But of course, there wasn't an exit door. Not even a doorway. Just earth. I'm pretty sure you know what a grave looks like. I floated up to the top of the grave and to my own surprise, poked my head right through it. Head sticking out of the ground, I looked around and could see the whole graveyard of Oak Wood Cemetery. It was as if it was the norm. The energy in motion traveled at a high frequency. Some sad weeping. Others joyfully excited. The rest just willingly accepting the fate of their destiny. Still they conversed and mingled as if it was a regularity. Angels came and went visiting graves. I guess sending direct messages down from God. Demons came and went as well visiting the graves from where you could hear screams of horror as souls were being tortured beneath their tombstones.

"Q, wats up, fool?" the same familiar voice that drew me out of my grave said. I looked to my right and wouldn't you know it. It was Burga.

I fully removed my soul's body from my grave and approached the soul of Burga. My longtime friend. My brother. We dapped up. We embraced. We hugged. "Brah, what the—" I said as we pulled away from each other. "Oops. Forgot I can't curse anymore."

Burga laughed. "I know, brah. That's how I was. It's easy to get used to though."

"I thought I wasn't gone ever get to see you again, brah."

"Who you telling? You was the first person I was looking for when I got to the other side and saw how it really was. Then I found out that you weren't even dead. Then soon after that I heard that you was on your way. At first I ain't know what to believe after already thinking that you was dead when you were still alive. I only accepted it as the truth when I saw them digging your grave. Right next to mine."

A white truck had pulled up at a short distance from our graves. The truck blared music through the speakers that you could hear clearly through the open windows. Some souls started dancing and jamming to the music. While the others were out right annoyed. "They say my whole city want me dead / Mama say I got a black cloud over my head / Load up them K's nigga, you know how we play it / Stop that rumor 'fore it even get to spread, ayy ayy ayy—" The lyricist expressed his pain over the chorus. Some people hopped out and instantly I knew who they were here for.

"Look like you got some visitors," I said to Burga. They came bearing gifts of flowers and a small statue angel.

"My sister, her husband, my momma, nieces and nephew. They always come through showing love. I wish I had a way of letting them know that it was received."

"Hey, Uncle!" the kids shouted with gleefulness as if they could see the presence of Burga. His nephew ran over to the balloons that were already pinned down in the ground to Burga's grave. He started to smack and punch them, playing Power Ranger, making sound effects with his mouth. "Watch this, Q." Burga was untying one of the strings of the balloons lose. It slowly rose up in the air. His nephew desperately tried to catch it before it was joining the clouds.

"Oops," the young boy said, almost hoping no one noticed.

"He do dat every time, "his older sister gave him up.

"Wat I tell you 'bout beatin' up my brotha's balloons?" Burga's sister asked her son after smacking him on the back of his head.

"Dats probably Burga ass doin' dat," Burga's mother assumed while busting out in a laugh.

"It probably is," his sister agreed. "His ass play too much." Burga and I shared a laugh as we watched the encounter.

"You got the little man in trouble," I said.

"He'll be alright. Let me see what they talking about though. I'll be back. Of course, I can't go nowhere anyway."

For what it was worth, I let Burga chill with his family. Meanwhile, I sat on the tombstone that held my name on it and took in more of the happenings that took place in the graveyard. Not a lot of human visitors came by, but a few did. I noticed a cream Audi A8 pull up with sparkling chrome wheels; it pulled up behind the white truck. The car was stylish and clean. Even the rubber on the tire glowed. Looked like something I wouldn't mind riding in. Both of the back doors flung wide open and the girls rushed out not even bothering to close the doors. It was De'Asia and De'Mia. I never expected there could be so many surprises after being surprised by death. "Y'all slow da fuck down!" Keyshia yelled to the running girls as she got out the driver's seat. "And stop walkin' ova dem people's graves. Damn it. Excuse me, Lord. Des kids, I swear." She closed the other car doors before meeting De'Asia and De'Mia at my grave.

"Hey, Daddy!" De'Mia smiled in a blush.

"Dad, I tried to tell Mommy dat we saw you but she don't wanna believe us though," De'Asia said to me.

"I did not say dat. I told y'all to ask him why he ain't come and see me," Keyshia clarified.

"Cuz, Mommy, I told you already," De'Mia reminded Keyshia. De'Asia laughed.

"Gurl, wateva. Ain't nobody listenin' to you!" Keyshia said.

"Well, you should." De'Mia halfway rolled her eyes. "I kno' everything." If I could cry tears, I'd be shedding them right now at this moment as I was hunched over the tombstone in the sitting position, bursting out in laughter. I always thought that life after death would be void. Empty, dark, sad, and lonely. Not saying that I would reject a second chance at life if given the opportunity. But this afterlife wasn't as bad and scary as humans make it seem.

"Don't listen to dem, Boo. You kno' yo' daughters crazy," Keyshia said to me.

"I know—I know," I said, trying to control my laughter as if she could hear my reply.

"They your kids," we miraculously said simultaneously. After that we shared a laugh. From there I was convinced that our synergy was somehow still connected. I reasoned that it could only be through the grace of God. I was thankful for his wonderful works of wonder. "Naw fo' real though, Boo. I miss you and love you so much. I wish things could be different. I wish we could go back to the beginning. I would have never allowed you to leave my side." Keyshia's smile quickly turned into a look of despair. She turned our energy sad. As if her emotion vibrated directly towards me. Wish I could tell her to remain happy so I could be happy. Let her know that I was fine. I wouldn't want her to live her life passing days in regret. That would only remind me of my neglect of responsibilities. Those days have passed and we can't get them back. The only moment we had was now. And if I only had this moment to have her in my presence, I was grateful.

"DeQuan. 'Q The Ghost' Anderson." Keyshia was now reading my tombstone out loud. "Loving father, lover, and friend. Gone before time." She paused and screwed her face up. "Gone before time." She repeated the last part. "Who in da hell put dis tombstone together and why in da hell would dey put some shit like dat on der?"

"I did," said a woman, walking up from the left of Keyshia's blindside, pushing a stroller. Even I was caught off guard by her mesmerizing presence.

Keyshia looked to her left, took a step back while using her right foot as a pivot, and stared. "And who da fuck is you?" Her tone was low, disrespectful, and definitely challenging. However, her eyes expressed a silent respect and admiration for the beauty that the woman possessed.

"My name is Dawn." She stuck her right hand out, and it alone spoke volumes. With its freshly French manicured finger nails. The tone of the colors said classy but still powerful. The sparkling tennis VVS diamond bracelet and matching cluster of a ring that I had bought her almost froze Keyshia's heart. She stared at the hand that still awaited her embrace and glanced at the baby that occupied the stroller. Her eyes widened for a quick shocking second as if she had been electrocuted by the sight of my son.

"Oh kayyy—" Keyshia said, ignoring Dawn's request for a hand shake but returning her eye contact.

"Look, Keyshia, at first I didn't kno'—"

"Hold up." Keyshia cut her off with the assistance of a raised hand. "And wat exactly is it dat you didn't kno' dat might involve me? Wat? Dat you was fuckin' my man?"

Dawn's face expressed the look of a person with a sudden broken heart. She should have expected this from Keyshia. I warned her time and time again before, although you could never prepare for the wrath of Keyshia. "Listen, please," Dawn pleaded respectfully.

"Umm hmm." Keyshia folded her arms, tilting her head.

"I had no idea, honestly. I would have never—"

"But you did. Wats yo' name again? Hmm, Dawn, you did it. But you kno' wat? It's done and you can't take it back." Keyshia glanced down into the car seat and stroller once more. "He looks so much like Q, it's unreal. At least you got to live da best years of his life wit'em. Meanwhile my foolish-in-love ass gottem through da struggle."

"No, dats far from da truth. It was a time I could have died jus' for being in the presence of dat man."

"Hmph. Serves you right I guess." Keyshia nonchalantly shrugged.

"Keyshia, I really don't want to do dis. Not here. Not now. Not at dis moment. Definitely not in front of the kids. And especially at a time of grievance. If you'll be able to find da strength and someday agree to it, maybe we can sit down and have a real conversation like grown women."

"Honestly, right now only God knows. But I can't say dat I won't at least think 'bout it. Besides, I really have no right to be mad at you. Regardless if you knew or not. Instead, I wish Q ass was here so I could take it out on him. Even buried in da grave, he still finds a way to burn up my soul." Keyshia was shaking her head, looking down at the tombstone.

"Gurl, dats Q ass fo' you. I tell you." Dawn agreed.

"You kno' you fo'got to put 'his' in front of *time* on da tombstone, right?" Keyshia asked with a slightly pointed finger.

"No. I kno' it says 'Gone Before Time', meanin' dat time doesn't actually hold you or keep you. Nor does it let you go because time doesn't exist. It's jus' a marker of events. Q's time isn't ova. He is eternal. He was passin' through dis phase of life. Now he's at da next phase. Similar to how we spend a phase as a seed. Spend a phase in da egg. Spend a phase in da womb."

"Oh well—" Keyshia said, sounding relieved that Dawn had shut up before she would have to cut her off again. "I hope he can hear me." She had no idea that she was staring right in the face of my ghost phase. "I'ma kick his ass if I eva get to catch back up wit his ass." I laughed and planted a cool kiss on her cheeks. She slightly shivered for a split second in the heat of eighty-three-degree weather.

Soon Dawn and Baby Q was pulling off in a Rolls Royce Dawn, arctic white. She had definitely embraced my taste of luxury. A few more moments had passed before my daughters and Keyshia went onto their way. I couldn't tell you how long because time really was expunged here. All we had was the sun and the moon. I was happy that I got to witness my children's mothers' first encounter. Especially since I wasn't man enough to make it happen myself when I was physically with them. Although Dawn had suggested it many times. And though I was happy, I wasn't sad when they parted ways either.

"It always feel good to have some people pull up through this joint every now and then. You got some beautiful kids too, Q." Burga was heading my way.

"Thank you, brah. Your family be turnt up, but they beautiful as well though."

"They crazy is what they are."

"Where everybody else at?" I asked of the ones that we've lost in the field of the projects.

"Well, Stan here. He over there." Burga indicated towards Stan's grave at the short distance on the other end of the same block we were on. "Streets here. The youngings Qua, Juwan, and Jo Jo here." Burga paused for a minute. There was a sentimental expression all over his face. "Reggie and Lil' Mark somewhere running with the demons."

"What?" I asked in disbelief. "But why?"

"Lil' Mark couldn't help it. It was too easy for them to snatch him. And Reggie wanted to go. Say he was trying to find a way to get Flex killed." I almost didn't want to hear the words that Burga verbalized but I wasn't surprised.

"But I thought that we had to stay at our graves with our bodies until they reincarnated back into the soils of the earth?"

"Yeah, but they never got a chance to make it to their graves. The longer their souls stay away from their graves, the longer their bodies would remain there, leaving their soul's bond to the earth. That's if they don't slip up and get burnt in the hell fire before Judgement Day arrives. All those demons do is promise false manipulations as if they could give us the life that we always wanted. Whole time though, they just trying to get they count up."

"Wat about Jay Jr? Where he at?"

"Cremated. At his mama's house."

"But how does that work?" I was curious.

"His body never got the chance to touch the earth. So his souls would have to stay with the ashes until they are set free."

Things were much more complicated now that I pondered on them. Make the concept of heaven and hell sound simple compared to all the *betweeness*. "Can we go over there?" I pointed across the field. "To holler at Stan?"

"You can go anywhere you want within these walls of this graveyard. It's like a force field for the souls along the walls. But I don't usually move around much. I'm either down there on my casket or chilling on my tombstone waiting on a visit."

"But why not move around some, mingle, if you still got that much of your free will?"

"Because, Q, I barely tipped the scale. I'd rather use my will to chill. Just because our bodies are buried don't mean that we're paralyzed from sin. We ain't make it to heaven yet."

"So you telling me that it ain't any souls in heaven right now?"

"I mean yeah. The Prophets. The Babies. The true saints. The ones that died for the cause of Allah. And the ones that was just about blameless from sin during their moments here on earth. I think the scale had to weigh at least seventy-seven percent of good deeds. Imagine that? Besides, Q, it's just as easy to get caught up out here as it is in the projects. Think about it, you smart. We got souls from all over the city, different projects, and sides all scattered out over a field full of graves. How you think that might turn out? If you don't stay out the way of mischief, you just might get back doored out here."

"Back doored?" My confusion was expanded. "But how?"

"Maine, some of these souls desperate. Know they destined for hell. And instead of trying to reverse their troubles, they looking to earn a favor from Satan. By tricking other souls, setting them up so demons can snatch them, brutality sacrificing them."

"Maine, this sounds just like the projects."

"Yeah, and sometimes it feels worst. Like jail. And just like jail the only thing you could do is wait to be judged and released. Just like life inside our bodies, this is just a phase on the stairway to heaven. And now that I know better and realize that I am still blessed with the will to do so, I'm stacking all good deeds just like I did my dollars and guns. That's the only way to buy you a ticket to heaven."

"But still though, you think it'd hurt just to go right there?" I gestured towards Stan's grave again.

"After all I just said? I ain't ever known you to be so hard-headed. Earnest, yes. But hard-headed. What? You incompetent?"

"Look the way things seeming it's a lot more to this other world outside of our old world—"

"You may be right," Burga cut me off. "But I don't want to find out."

"You say you want to stack good deeds? Well, what's a better way to do that than warring with the force of evil?"

"I'd rather take the easy route."

"What about Reggie and Lil' Mark?"

"What about them? They chose their own destiny."

"Maybe they don't know any better. Never seen another way."

"Q, I'm really starting to hate you, brah."

"You shouldn't do that. Hate is a sin."

"What are you up to? I know you, Q. There's something up your sleeve." I looked at my arms that were just about see-through. "Well, you know what I mean." I remained silent for a while. "See, I knew it," Burga elaborated, sensing that I had something on my mind. "What is it?"

Remember earlier when I warned you to be careful of what you asked for? Well, Burga asked for it. And in a world where good deeds was the money and sin was the debt, I refused to lie. "I want to try and see if I can try to save Flex."

"What?" Burga asked, enthused with frustration. "You must have forgot that he is the reason why my soul is removed from my body and my body is buried in dirt."

"First of all, it was the decree of Allah."

"Wat?"

"Plus the way I heard the story, you basically jumped in front of the gun trying to stop him from killing Hawk. Who knows, maybe that was the deed that tipped your scale."

"True but that last part is an assumption."

"And maybe it really wasn't Flex that killed you."

"That's a delusional statement."

"No. Not really. I seen it for myself. Demons surrounds him in temptation. He's wickedly influenced by them."

"Still not convinced."

"Luke 15-7 says 'I tell you that in the same way there will be more rejoicing in heaven over one sinner who repents than over ninety-nine righteous persons who do not need repentance."

"How you—"

"There was a time I had to study all the scriptures of the Holy Books in order to find my way out."

"To find your way out what?"

"A cave."

"What?" Now Burga was the one looking confused. Who are you?"

"That's another story. Off topic. Listen, the point I'm trying to make is, what if we were the ones to help him towards repenting? Don't you think there would be some good deeds in it for us for guiding the lost sheep home?"

"What type of genius plan do you have for us to do that? How can us simple souls war against those devilish demons? They be poofing and popping in and out of thin air. They got all these weird weapons and can show up in all type of convincing disguises. Plus we outnumbered by an enormous ratio. What do we have?"

"An army of angels. The best military ever designed by the Great Creator himself. I seen this one angel named ZQ take on multiple demons by herself. Then when she did call for help there were only a slight number of angels and many demons. Either they got scared and poofed away or they were wiped out, turned into ashes. The angels will fight for us, protect us. We do have the benefit of being good souls."

"You don't think that God doesn't know that we are plotting?"

"Yep. I'm certain that he knows. He's All Seeing, All Knowing. But maybe it was part of our destiny. By what other means would we still have our free will?"

"I still don't know about this, Q."

"Look, brah, I'm ready go over there to holler at Stan and maybe see who else I can find. You can chill here and I'll check back with you when I get back."

"That's if you make it back." His words caught up with me from a distance as I was already in pursuit. "Q!" Burga had called out to me with a tone full of concerned passion. I only stopped to turn around halfway. "Hold on, brah. I'm coming with you!" he said, catching up to me. "I can't believe you got me doing this. You always find a way to get people under your spells of heroics. I'm telling you now, brah, nothing better happen. We need to make sure we make it back to our graves. God forgives but I don't. You gone forever owe me for this. And don't come up on any bright ideas while we over here either." As we traveled, Burga ceaselessly babbled.

Chapter Seven

Flex Back in the Field

I walked out one of the back hallways on the one way around Jackson Ward in the Gilpin Court projects. Pulling the hoodie of my Carhartt coat over my head, I sheltered it from the rain. Thunder roared almost as if it was a warning of a wrath to come. Even in the darkened sky you could tell that the clouds were heavy. They gathered like an angry mob, causing an intense down pour of rain. I knew I had to make it to my destination quick or I'll be soaking wet. Ready to weather the weather, I had my ACG's laced prepared to walk through the storm.

Watching my footing, I hurriedly descended the few steps traveling off the porch. Pow! Ping! "Wat da fuck!" A bullet had flown past me, barely missing my backside before smacking into the black iron gate. Nervous, to say the least and definitely caught off guard, I slightly struggled to slide my Glock .40 out of the pockets of my coat. Strangely a rarity had happened. The gun had gripped onto the inside of my pocket somehow. As if something was preventing me from whipping it out. Finally, when I was able to, *pow, pow! Boc, boc, boc, boc, boc! Pow, pow! Pow!* The shots were coming from my right side. While swinging the pistol in that direction with my right hand, I looked over to take a glance. The image of Reggie and Lil' Mark startled me damn near half to death. It was if a bullet had already smacked my chest and pierced into my heart. I could reason with Reggie even though I had no idea that it was him that I chopped down in that Rolls Royce. For the life of me though, I could not figure out why Lil' Mark was slinging shots at my head.

Unconsciously I dropped the gun. Subconsciously I ran weaving in a wave, hoping that the rain would be the only thing to leave me wet. Consciously I searched for an escape route. Couldn't be a hallway. That would be a trap. Straight ahead of me across the street was a fence that was on the border of the highway. Maybe if I made the leap in time, I could make it down the hill and travel alongside the sea of cars. It was well after midnight. Traffic was light. *Pow, pow, pow, pow, pow! Boc, boc, boc!* Them niggas was on my ass. I ain't gone lie though, knowing these two steppers the way I did, it was odd that I wasn't hit yet.

I was approaching the edge of the building fast. Figured I'd round the corner to buy me some time. My foot splashed into a deep puddle of water which rose so high that I could fill the liquid drenching my sock. No, wait, that was blood. I was hit in the foot. I ran with a limp. I wrenched from the pain, but I guess the rush of adrenaline wouldn't allow me to feel it. A car horn honked. Sitting at the edge of the street was a SRT Demon. Qua and Jo Jo sat in the front seat. The back door opened up and out hopped JuWuan. "Come on, brah, hurry up!" He waved me over. A sudden sense of safety washed over me. I can't say why. For none of this was making sense. But I wondered where Q was and why he wasn't here to help me. All my life I had known him to have my back. I really wish he was here now. Fully coming around the corner, two figures stood awaiting in the rain. They both were shadowed by this one huge umbrella. It kept both of them protected from the rain. Dry as a desert in the Middle East standing in a pair of rain boots. The umbrella lifted a little as I damn near ran into them. Their faces were revealed. It was Q and Burga. I froze. Stopped dead in my tracks. From the consequences of that, Reggie and Lil' Mark was able to catch up with me. Their footsteps splashed water against the muddy grass. And just like the foundation of the earth, I knew this shit was about to get dirty. To my surprise, both Reggie and Lil' Mark looked surprised at the sights of Q and Burga. The pairs from both sides locked eyes with the one standing across from them. The vibe was like they were speaking without the use of words. Reggie and Lil' Mark began to simultaneously put their guns down. "Flex," Q said, requesting my attention. I took my eyes away from my attempted murders and looked over to Q who now stood with his hand held out. Contemplating on its meaning, I hesitated. Was this a trap? Or an offering of help? Could I not trust my own brother, even after all I've done to him?

"Flex!" Jo Jo yelled out the window of the car. "Behind you." Quickly I turned back to the two who tried to kill me only a few seconds ago. Reggie had his gun back raised. As I turned, the cold steel was met with the temple of my forehead. I'd rather it be him than the opps, I guess.

"Flex! Wat da fuck is wrong wit you?" I woke up in the back seat of a cutlass from screaming sounds of Lil' Shawty's voice. "Get yo' ass up. You back der screamin', cryin', laughin', and shit in yo' sleep. How da fuck you go from cryin' to laughin'?"

"Somebody probably was trying to kill his ass," Two concluded while chuckling an innocent laugh.

"Well, it ain't us. Get up though fo' real, we here. Ion kno' des people."

I sat up in the back seat stretching my legs as far as I was allowed to. "Shidd, Ion kno' des ma'fucka's either." I was now rubbing my eye with the palm of hand. Shaking my head side to side, I tried to empty out the nightmare of this beautiful morning out of my head. The sun was ablaze, though I could tell that it had just awoken. Meaning it was a little after sunrise. In the middle of this month of May, that calculation would add up to about six o'clock in the morning. The sky was clear with the exception of a few clouds. Birds soared, allowing the wind to propel their direction. We rolled past a welcoming sign that read: West Side Village. The cars slowed and rolled over a speed bump continuing on down a steady but long hill. Kids zoomed past the car going down the hill on their bikes, purposely popping their bikes into the air over the speed bump. The car remained at a low speed, approaching speed bump after speed bump. "Where da fuck we at?" I asked, confused as hell.

"Ion kno'," Lil' Shawty replied from behind the wheel. "Dis da address we were 'possed to come to."

"I thought we was 'possed to go to da country or somewhere?"

"Dis is da country. You would have known dat if you weren't back der cryin' and shit." Two chuckled again at Lil' Shawty's comment. "Dis shit was full of none but trees for miles 'til we got here." She said that as if she could hardly believe it herself. "Trust me. I think dis is da last place yo' ass need to be. It's only 'possed to be a steppin' stone."

"Why da fuck des kids ain't somewhere gettin' ready fo' school or some?" I asked.

"It's Saturday, fool."

"Still, it's early as a bitch." A little boy rolled alongside the car on his bike, traveling at the damn speed as us. He peered through the car, trying to get a peek at who we were. I frowned at him for his nosiness. He raised his middle finger up, stuck his tongue out, and sped off ahead.

"Aww, bad ass lil' fucka," Two said in shock.

"I'ma beat his lil' ass," I promised.

"You don't even kno' dat boy," Lil' Shawty reminded me.

"He better hope Ion ever see his ass again out here." Analyzing the rest of the kids, I noticed that damn near most of them were barefoot. The soles of their foot just as black as the skin in their face. The little boys and girls alike. If not for wife beaters all the boys were shirtless. They were claiming their manhood by exposing their bird chest. I can't say that I didn't respect the pride though. Besides, they looked happy as Willy Wonka when he got to show off Hot Chocolate Factory. As if they were living their best lives. Seems as if they couldn't wait for the sun to pop out so they could grab their bikes and head for the hills. Reminded me off my childhood days that I suddenly missed so much.

I looked around the rest of the neighborhood. Brown and burgundy bricks built up the structures of the apartments. If I could eliminate the geographical differences, it may be plausible to say that this was the projects. Somewhere ducked off in the middle of I don't know where. Though there had to be more, I thought. Who else would they rival with? Where else would the niggas that was cast out of their hood go? To the woods camped out with the deers and bears? Lil' Shawty pulled up and parked in a parking space. "This da address right here." She pointed at the doors straight ahead of us sitting side by side. "Da one da right." Nobody moved. Lil' Shawty and Two turned around to the back of the car to look at me. "Well?" Lil' Shawty asked. "After you."

"Why I gotta go?"

"Cuz dis yo' people spot, duhhh!" Two said, smacking her gum. I picked one of my pistols up from off the floor. One with the silencer screwed to it. I dropped the clip to check the count. Eleven plus the one in its head made twelve. "You really think you gone need dat?" Lil' Shawty questioned.

"You kno'." I slammed the clip back into the gun. "Y'all said des niggas 'posed to be some brothas of mine, right?" Lil' Shawty looked on. "Well, if dats true, da niggas might be crazy or untrustworthy. Either way, I ain't lookin' to take a gamble on'em."

"Boy, wateva," Lil' Shawty said. "Ain't nobody untrustworthy but yo' ass. Get yo' ass to dat door so we can kno' if we can get out dis car or do we need to keep movin' further down South."

"I'm gettin' sick of yo' mouth fo' real, bitch." I lifted my body from the seat of the car, tucking the extended muzzle into my pants, resting it on my thigh. Held tightly by my LV belt. Two laughed again. "Fuck you keep laughin' at?" I asked her as I opened the car door. She laughed some more. I slammed the door shut. "Bitches startin' to think I'ma joke or some." I mumbled to myself on the way to the apartment door. "Dis shit ain't no fuckin' game." I met the door and rapped on it with my knuckles. No answer. I created another rhythm of knocks at the door. Still nothing though. Then I found myself banging on it with my fist. Same shit, nothing. Feeling defeated, I turned to leave the door. "Bitches probably don't even got da right address." I continued talking to myself on my way to the car. Until I heard the lock of the apartment door clicking. As I turned around to face it, I found the door swinging open inwardly. A nigga with a dark complexion, six nappy cornrows to the back, standing at about 5'8, posted in the doorway. He wore a pair of black Nike slippers and the basketball shorts to match. In a split second a big ass Red Nose Pitbull was speeding towards the door at a rapid tempo. Find a word of your own to use and replace it with fear. That's what I thought I felt. I stepped back a few feet as I whipped out the pistol.

"Aye, Honey! Chill! Sit!" the owner of the apartment and the dog shouted. The Pitbull covered in an almond brown fur did as it was commanded but stared at me with its lime green eyes awaited any wrong movement from its imposer. "Aye, brah," dude in the door turned his attention towards me now. "I swear to God, brah, if you shoot my fuckin' dog it'll be a mistake you'll never get to learn from." Since the dog had arrived in my presence it was hard for me to take my eyes off the animal that resembled a mid-aged lioness. Once I finally picked up the courage to do so, I looked directly into the eyes of his owner. Immediately I knew. It was undeniable. I gave the dude a perplexed look. He returned the expression.

"Babe!" I heard a voice coming from the back of the apartment. A quick gander past the dude's head and I caught a woman coming down the stairs wearing a pink robe carrying a snub nose revolver in hand. "Fat!" she said, getting louder and closer.

Fat, I assumed his name to be, looked at me up and down with a look of both confusion and understanding. "Yeah, Babe!" he called slightly over his shoulder. "Everything good." Fat took an extra second to ponder before he spoke. "Put dat gun up," he said. "You causin' an unnecessary scene out'cha early in da mornin' fo' none. Which one are you? Q or Flex?"

I was stunned but managed to answer. "Flex," I said, "How'd you kno'—"

"I figured. Where Q at?" Fat asked, peeking over my shoulder, trying to get a view of the car behind me.

Putting my head down in shame and tucking the pistol into my pants, I reluctantly replied, "Q couldn't make it."

Fat looked disappointed. "Dey wit you?" He directed to Lil' Shawty and Two sitting in the car.

"Yeah."

"Tell 'em come in. Y'all good." I hesitated to turn around, having no trust at all in Fat's loyal companion. "Honey." Fat snapped his fingers and pointed towards the back. "Go lay." Honey did as she was told with full comprehension. I turned towards the car and waved the ladies out of the car. They did as I suggested without having to be told. Fat laughed lightly. "One thing 'bout dem bitches, dey be loyal as a ma'fucka." The way he just compared his dog to my two partners in crime was my second confirmation that he was definitely one of the brothers that I was looking for.

Seated in the living room of the apartment, I admired the wonderful finesse of decoration. It defined richness in rachetness. Pride in blackness. Screamed peace. And honorably demanded respect. I sat on the green suave couch overflooded with golden leather pillows, in between Lil' Shawty and Two. The woman in the robe returned from upstairs. She'd replaced the robe for a pair of sweet pants and a white tee. In her hands, she replaced the gun for a baby. "Boo, dey woke Fat Baby up." From other assumption of mine, I was guessing that the lady was Fat Baby's mother. She walked over to the other couch and took a seat beside Fat.

"Dis my wife, Flex. And our son." *Wife*? I pondered on Fat's words inside the skull of my head. I was almost sure that he was using that word in a slang sense. Until I sat my eyes on their fingers. The evidence was the gold wedding bands on both of their fingers. On top of that, her finger had an additional glistening diamond ring. If I had to estimate, I would say the cost was anywhere from thirty to forty bands. That indicated money or love, or maybe a combination of both. "Her name is Moony, y'all can call her Moon. As you heard already, our son name is Fat Baby." If I wasn't sitting right here in Fat's face and was to just hear his voice over the phone along with the mention of his name, I would have sworn that I was actually talking to a fat nigga. Ironically, though, the nigga was skinny and smaller than me. Moon was white with a dark suntan. Her swag screamed *black* though.

"How do you kno' me?" I asked, actually speaking for the first time since we sat down.

"You my brotha, dummy." Just from the short time of being around this nigga, I could tell that Fat had a slick mouth. That might be a problem for the both of us.

"But how do you kno' dat?" I humbly tried my best to stick to the script.

"Pops told me 'bout you and Q a long time ago. He even told me to get ready because one day whenever you and Q got tired of running da streets, dat it was a strong possibility dat y'all would somehow someway find y'all way to us. Guess Q still having fun out der in dem streets."

"Naw," I defended Q remorsefully. Every time Fat mentioned Q's name, a wave of unwanted emotions were washing over my heart. "Q not in da streets no more."

"Oh yeah. Where da fuck da nigga at den? Why he ain't come wit you? Wat? Da nigga too good fo' da country or some?"

"Q in da grave." I summed up all the answers to Fat's questions into one. Fat was trapped into silence. Moon looked burdened as well. Fat Baby outburst with a whine of cries. His mother bounced him up against her breast, attempting to soothe his acquired vibrations of our mood. "I think he would have loved to be here." Matter of fact, I'm certain. This was Q's plan from the get-go. It's been almost a year since I betrayed him and stopped him from proceeding. Now here I was, in the same shoes that I knocked him out of.

"Damn, dats fucked up. Even though I never met him, I was lookin' forward to da day dat I would get da chance too. I kinda feel cheated dat da opportunity was snatched away from me. Dis is not to seem rhetorical but how did he die?"

"He got shot. Two to da head."

"Da killa?"

"Dead. He ain't last a minute. I made sure of dat."

"So you was der?" I just stared at Fat, refusing to answer the question. "Yeah, you right," he said, understanding my gesture. "So I take it now you on da run and dats wat landed you here? Wat y'all 'possed to be though?" He pointed between Lil' Shawty and Two who sat on both sides of me. "Bonnie, Bonnie, Clyde? See, Boo, I told you dat sista wife shit was normal." Moon tapped her husband on the back end of his shoulders while rolling her eyes.

"Wat 'bout yo' brotha? I thought it was two of y'all?"

"Our brotha," Fat corrected. "Yeah, we can go pull up on him. Give me a minute to get myself together."

Chapter Eight

Q

Gathering Good Graces

As Burga and I traveled through the field of graves, I became conscious of the troubles that threatened our invisible existence. As he said, they did; demons swooped down from the sky, intruding into certain graves. Passing by, loud shrilly cries could be heard from souls being tortured by the demons who hunted their graves. On one occasion I overheard the conversation between a demon and a naive soul. The soul was being tempted to leave its grave in order to indulge in jestful frolic. The soul gave in to the dream it was having. With the given permission the demon wrapped his arms around the soul and together they vanished. Another conversation I caught notice of was in the manner of a plot. "You still gone do dat for me, right?" the demon asked, voice as conniving as a politician trying to convince the public out of a vote.

"Hell yeah! I got you, fool!" the soul assured. "I ain't like dat nigga when I was alive anyway. I died tryin' to kill dat nigga. So, shit, you doin' me a favor. I'ma play it cool wit da nigga and when da time is right you can pull up and do you. Jus' make sure when you handle yo' business you come back and get a nigga out dis graveyard. I'm tryin' to go out into da world and cause hell wit you. Hunt some peoples dreams and shit like Freddie Krueger. Get some payback." The demon and soul laughed in heinous harmony.

"You kno' I'ma come back and get you. We can fuck a lot of shit up. Jus' hurry da fuck up. You never kno' when the trumpet might blow announcin' da day of judgement." They dapped up. The demon shot up and out over the wall.

"What happen to rest in peace?" I wondered out loud indirectly.

"Guess peace is earned," Burga said. We reached the grave of Stan. I stood facing his tombstone. After a foolish attempt, I realized that I was not permitted access into his grave. "Knock," Burga said. I showed a look of confusion. "On the tombstone," he clarified. I did, waited, and repeated. Soon Stan's ghostly head was protruding out of the ground. He sat his sights on my being and thrusted his translucent body from out of the dirt.

"What's up, Q!?" Stan spoke jovially. "I see you still kno' how to find your way to my door mat."

"Yeah, brah, I need you, Stan," I answered.

"That's always," Stan said. "Why switch up now, right?"

"What happened? How did you end up here?" I changed the motive of my reason for being here. The last time I had seen Stan, I had popped up at his crib one morning to take him out shopping. A small expression of my appreciation for all the things that he'd done for me. Mainly the guidance I received from his sincere advice. That morning, though, I found Stan's lifeless body peacefully wrapped up in the sheets of his bed. No signs of struggle. No wounds indicating injury. No evidence of murder at all. It was as if God had sent the angels to remove his soul while he was fast asleep.

"Guess it was my time, Q. You know? Whatever my purpose to be on earth, I guess, was fulfilled. Only God knows. Even the doctors were lost as to what my cause of death was. They just assumed that my heart stopped but there were no signs of a heart attack. All I know is that I'm here now. The best part of it all is that I won't be here for long. I got a ticket straight to heaven. Even though I may land on the fourth heaven, I can still work my way up to higher ranks. Right now all I have to do is guard my physical body until it returns to its original form, steer clear of all these demons, and for an angel to come through and give me a lift." Stan's soul ascendance into heaven sounded so promising that I started to feel bad for coming to his grave. "What is it, Q? I know that face when I see it in any lifetime."

"I don't know, Stan. After hearing all of that, I kind of feel selfish for coming over here bothering you with my problems."

"Okay, so it's obvious that you ain't take the risk of making your way over here just to say hello. But now since you're here I think you should remain courageous and at least propose your overture. It's not like bothering me with your problems ever stopped you before. Besides, if there's something that I could help you with, I'll be more than willing to. Just as long as it's nothing that would put me in harm's way."

"Well, actually, Stan, I don't know exactly what it is that I'll need from you right now. I know what I want to do though."

"And what's that?"

"Save Flex," I vented vulgarly.

"Always the impossible with you, huh, Q?" Burga laughed lowly at Stan's comment.

"Nothing is impossible, Stan. Everything is nothing because everything came from it."

"Maybe you should have gone to college when you had spirit in your body. Maybe then you wouldn't have been in the grave so early." Burga laughed a little louder this time. "And since you know everything about nothing why do you persist to seek assistance?"

"A collective conscious is always better than one. And in the words of the genius Albert Einstein *'No problem can be solved from the same level of consciousness that created it.*"

"What?" Stan and Burga challenged collectively in confusion.

"Look, I know Flex seem destined for hell. But there's an alarming intuition silently telling me that he can be saved, and that we can and will give him help."

"Why don't you just leave that up to God?" Stan wanted to know.

"Exactly," Burga agreed.

"How do you not know that God is using us to do that job?"

"So you telling me that God wanted us dead to save Flex?"

"I don't know what God wants other than for us to worship him. But like I told Burga, what better way to do that than by guiding a lost soul back to the straight path?"

"Ayee!" a different voice called, approaching from a distance. "What y'all got going on over here?" The voice was another familiar one. I turned around and confirmed that it was Streets to me. "Even to the grave. I wish I would have told you to live your life. I guess destiny is unstoppable.

"This fool talking about roaming the earth to fight off demons to help Flex," Burga announced. We waited on a response.

"No one can help Flex unless he is willing to help hisself. Not even God is willing to help the unwilling," Streets professed.

"Right," Stan confessed. "But don't forget this is Flex we talking about. He's in love with the life he lives. I don't think he would—"

"I seen him cry." I cut Stan off. The three loyalists amongst me looked surprised just by the confession of me witnessing a tear in Flex's eye. "Allah said that a mustard seed of faith could change the heart towards the light. If that tear I saw meant what I think it did, then that may be just enough water to extinguish the burning fires of his sin."

"You seen him cry?" Burga asked for assurance.

"I seen him cry." I provided the reply with certitude.

"I don't know," Burga said. I could feel his vibrations being lifted to a higher frequency. "There might be some hope for the looney."

"Not only did he cry. He even stayed back to bury my body. Not even Cain did that for Abel," I added.

"Okay, but even if we did agree to help, how will we be able to get it done? How can we get into Flex's head or even his heart for that matter? How can we show him something that he can't see? And aside from all that, how can we go against the odds with just the four of us?" Burga dreadfully inquired.

"What y'all on? We trying to find something to get into ourselves." Creeping up on my backside was Qua with Juwan and Jo Jo on each side of him. "Q, what's up? What you still doing in the graveyard? I would have thought that your body been had returned back to the dirt by now."

"I just got here." I answered Qua's question.

"Huh?" Juwan asked, obviously lost from my reply.

"That's crazy," said Jo Jo.

"You just got here?" Qua expressed his bafflement. "Where you been at the whole time?"

"It's like a long, almost unbelievable story. But right now, I'm trying to come up with a way to save Flex from ending up here with us. Or, if he do have to come here, hopefully he'd have his good deeds out weighing his bad." I was trying to sound convincing to this nonsensical idea.

"You said you was just getting here, right?" Qua reminded me.

"Yeah."

"So that mean you haven't been on the tour yet?"

"What tour?" Now I was in a disoriented mind frame.

"All man," Streets interposed. "You haven't been on the tour yet?" he asked. "That explains why he's still full of so much bravery."

"Yeah Q, it's hot in hell," Burga said.

"And terrifying," Jo Jo added.

"Heaven is definitely the place to be," Stan authenticated.

"So y'all telling me y'all been to hell?" I searched for clarity.

"Hell no!" Streets, Qua, and Jo Jo denied.

"They don't take you inside of hell. You fly over it and then go through a sort of scared straight situation at the gates," Burga said.

"Yeah, and just being around the gates of hell is just about enough heat to melt the aura of a soul. And just for that reason is why I sit inside my grave until it's time for an angel to take me back up to the heavens where the origins of love reside!" Stan interpreted. "But knowing you the way that I'm sure I know you, Q, you'll still have to go and see for yourself. Despite what the six of us right here trying to tell you."

"Yeah, you definitely know him," Streets admitted. "He listens but only through the confirmation of experience. You know that I would never intentionally mislead you, Q. But get back with me after you go on your tour. I'll see then if you still talking cuckoo." Streets was leaving.

"Yeah, I'm not sure about this one, Q," Stan said. "I'm just trying to rest in peace, brah. If it's safe and sound, then I'm down. But what you trying to do, I'm pretty sure it's risky. Love y'all but I'm gone." Stan entered his grave.

"Told you," Burga told me.

"I'll figure it out," was all I had to say.

Chapter Nine

Flex

Band of Brothers

Instead of the front door, we exited the apartment of Fat's through a patio. It led us to the other end of the apartment building. Which landed us to another parking lot. Two, Lil' Shawty, Fat, and I hopped into a Ford F-250 Roush Super Duty Powerstroke. I assumed that it belonged to Fat. He expertly handled it like the owner. Moon, Fat Baby, and Honey stayed back at the apartment. Fat suggested that Lil' Shawty and Two stay back as well. He said that they would be safe there and that I could trust his word. Even though I didn't have a reason to, I doubted it. The reason I dragged my tagalongs with me was because I didn't really trust them.

"A nigga needed love, was motivated, that kept me above / Nigga let off sixty, ain't hit none, I kno' he a strubb / Straight cash, paper tags, patience low as my brake pads / Talk behind my back, act like you love me, wit yo' fake ass /" Fat played a rapper with an unfamiliar voice that advocated adversity through the banging speakers. The sound, the words of the message, the pain, and the ambition caught my attention. It sparked my will to overcome.

I waved for Fat's attention as he steered the wheel through the country roads. He turned the music down low enough for my voice to be heard. "Who is dis?" I asked, curious to know the rapper.

"A nigga name YG Teck. Dude from Baltimore. He be talkin' dat shit. You ain't never heard of him befo'?" Fat returned the questioning around on me.

"Hell naw," I admitted. "He a'ight though."

Fat turned the music back up and rapped along with the song. "Dis a gutta run, dats my brotha like my mother son /..." Fat reached over and tapped my shoulder with his back hand. "...I was behind movin' forward, but I wanted to get better / You a loser if you quit, don't no hustla settle / You gotta leave some niggas behind when you upping yo' level / Keep goin' you kno' dem underdogs turn into legends? Bet it all on my grind, I be pushin' myself / You really got dis shit in you, why you lookin' fo' help? / if you don't believe in yo' self, den how you gone get better? / Truth is you kno' dem underdogs turn into legends /... I told you ova and ova again/'" The song faded out with a marvelous melody until another banger came on by the same artist.

The ride was somewhat long. I'd say about a good forty minutes. Within that time, I probably saw about ten cars in motion and enough trees to build a city full of cottages. I watched the woods with intense attentiveness just waiting for a bear to pop out. Never happened though. Just a deer on the side of the rode that dashed back into the woods as if it was a criminal on the block ducking twelve. We turned into a graveled paved driveway. At the top sat a big beautiful white house. On the porch sat a Caucasian older couple. They waved and smiled at the truck as it was passing by. Fat tapped the horn twice in response and continued to carefully cruise down the pathway. It was a slow, quiet, and long drive. On the way down the travel, to the right was one of those cottages that I was talking about earlier. It looked like something out of the 1800's. Abandoned, yet still livable. A small pond complemented the front yard of the cottage. Further down to the left was a trail off to I don't know where. All I know is that I lost sight of the path as it slithered off deep into the woods.

About five minutes later—well, maybe it was three, the driveway that was mostly closed in by woods on both sides was now opening up to what to me seemed like a whole new world. It was definitely something I've never seen before. An acreage of land. I'm talking acres on top of acres by the tens. To the right was a barn yard that obviously was adjoined to the barn. In the yard were four beautiful well taking care of horses. They sported manes that a few bitches in the projects I knew would pay thousands of dollars for. About twenty feet away from the barn was another one of those cottages. It was a little better up kept with a trio of old school automobiles parked in the front of it. The exterior of the cars were pre-served as if they had never been driven before. The models were old but yet the cars still looked brand new as if we were living in the year they were built. One was a 1966 Chevy Nova SS with a gun metal gray metallic paint job. The other was a 1967 Pro Touring Mustang Fast Back, painted in my favorite color—red. The last one was 1969 Camaro RS/SS Dupont with a chrome orange metallic color. I had a secret love for cars. Like a child at Chuck E. Cheese, I loved to play behind the wheel. On the side of the cottage was a Hauler Tow Truck. An International 4300 all-black. May have been made in the year 2013 or '14. Quickly a questioning thought swept through my mind but I let it go just as quick as it came.

Around the area where the driveway was finally about to come to an end, begun a large field raising crops of corn, beets, all types of greens, and rows of other growing foods that I couldn't identify with as we rode by. Straight ahead of us was a long and wide one-story house, although it was obvious that a basement sat underneath it. The structure was unique and beautiful. The porch wrapped around the back of the house going towards my left. Fat parked the truck, and swung his door open. "Dis yo' brotha's house?" I was prying.

"Our brotha," Fat corrected again as he grabbed his phone out of the cup holder. "Naw. Dis da Fam's house."

"Da Fam's?" I was kind of thinking out loud before certainly directing my question towards Fat. "Who is da fam?"

Fat paused from tapping his thumbs across the screen of his phone and looked over to me as if I was dumb. "You don't kno' wat family is?" he asked in a sense of disbelief.

"Ohh—Da family's house," I said only halfway understanding. If this was the family's house and I was family, then technically this was *our* house too. The misunderstanding came in when I had realized that I spent all of my life in the projects while having unknown options the whole time.

"Big Brah say he on da way now. He'll be here fast. Da nigga drive like lunatic." Fat looked towards the back of the truck at Lil' Shawty and Two. "Y'all don't talk much huh?" They looked at me. Two snapped a pop from her bubble gum.

"Naw, dey jus' takin' it all in like me. Da last couple days fo' dem has been exhausting. After that long drive dey probably need some rest and food."

"Already den, say no more. We got two showers. Dey can use dem both. We keep plenty of spare clothes. I'm pretty sure dey will be able to find some dat fit. We got four bedrooms, five beds. All of them are comfortable, so just find one to lay yo' head in. Da food is plentiful as well as you can see already. You ain't gotta worry 'bout dem tryin' to run off or none of dat. And I'm tellin' you now, if dey do try to I ain't chasing after dey ass. Plus anyway it ain't nowhere to go. I give dem five minutes in dem woods befo' dey asses runnin' back."

"Naw," I slurred. "Dey ridas. I trust 'em." The former statement was the truth. The latter was a prevarication.

"Already, lil' brah, I'ma take yo' word. It's yo' world. Let's go though."

"Lil' brah?" I asked for verification.

"Yeah, nigga, lil' brah. It's big brah, me, Q, and den you. Dats da order of our births. Pops made us a few years befo' he moved up to Richmond. He left mom and us behind. He wanted us to stay back. He was only 'possed to go up der to make some money moves. Even though he did, in da process he ended up making Q and you. He got so caught up in dat street life, dat even when he did come back, he'd drop money off, buy land and property, head back into da city. Pops was strangely open but secretive at da same time. Fo' da longest we knew nothing of Q's and your existence. I'm positive dat wasn't due to any neglect. Pops definitely loved y'all 'til death. I jus' think dat he dreaded causin' pain to mom's—well, my mama's fragile heart. Dey got married at da age of eighteen—"

"Pops was married?" I had to cut Fat off so I could slide the question in.

"Yeah, he died a married man. My mother's a widow." I contemplated on the fact that Pop's was a straight fucking player. He had married Fat's mother, fell in love with Q's, and was completely wide open off of mine. I was clearly starting to see which side of my DNA I had got my fucked-up conduct from. Seems as if my mama had a knack for fucking people's lives up. Sad to say, but I developed that quality quite well myself. "Anyway though 'bout six months befo' Pops was killed, he came and enlightened us all 'bout you and Q's whereabouts. He told us dat y'all knew nothing 'bout us while at da same time orderin' dat if y'all ever found y'all way to us fo' us to welcome y'all wit open arms. It was like Pops knew he was on his way to da exit of dis world. I don't kno' if he was into some fucked up shit in da streets or wat but—"

"Do you kno' how he died?" I had my version of the story but wanted to pick Fat's brain.

"Ion kno', brah. I heard a handful of stories. First I heard it was a shoot-out. Then I heard it was a robbery. Another story I heard was a triangular love affair gone wrong. All I knew fo' sure was dat he was gone. I could feel it. Ever since den, I've been waitin' fo' da day I could meet my other brothas. I guess meetin' one is better dan meetin' neither. Hopefully Q and Pops are watchin' ova us. But since you here it's time to fulfill my promise to Pops."

Fat hopped his skinny five-foot eight frame out this big ass truck and I found it humorous how his body closely resembled a thinner version of Q. Right before he slammed his door, he blew a whistling sound from his lips using two fingers for assistance. On call, four dogs came charging around the corner of the porch. The two Cocker Spaniels, one black the other white, were so small amongst the accelerated Pitbulls that I almost missed them. The Pits made it to Fat first, leaping off the porch, not even touching one of the seven steps. The first one to Fat was a blue pit covered in a shiny coat of grey fur with spikes of dark blue swoops. The dog jumped up towards Fat and eagerly stood on his hind legs. The belly of the pit was a pond of white fur. "Hey, Vick! Wats up, my boy? You always miss me da most, huh?" I heard Fat express through the rolled down windows. Honestly, it was hard to tell who missed who more. Fat was just as happy as the dogs. He was an obvious dog lover. The second pit approached Fat and demanded attention of its own. It was a red nose pit with striking colours on its fur. Mostly tan but other combinations of colors such as dark brown, black, white, and cream was aligned in strokes of its fur. "Hey, Thunder. You been a good boy?" Soon the Cocker Spaniels were catching up. They were barking with a loud aggression. Those little dogs had big hearts expressing no fear around the bigger dogs. Fat scooped down to their level. "Wats up, Salt and Pepper? Y'all hungry? Ready to eat?" For a minute it was as if Fat was in another world as he playfully enjoyed being in the company of the dogs. I almost thought that he forgot all about us. "Y'all ain't gotta be scared," he finally addressed us. "Dey don't kno' y'all so dey gone want to get a scent. But once I tell 'em wat it is, y'all gone be good." He spoke of the pets as if they were humans.

A few moments later, we were entering the house. After Fat took the dogs to the back porch to feed them, he escorted Lil' Shawty and Two to the two separate bathrooms. The sun was already heating up the earth's atmosphere while the air blew crisp. Fat and I sat on the front porch. He twisted up a *Backwood* while I mentally took in this twisted situation that I called my life. I found it funny that all my life I tried to play big brother to Q only to find out that I was the youngest of them all. Finalizing the finishing touches on the blunt, Fat fired up the stick. He took his share of hits and passed it over to me. "Look like you need some of dis shit," he said between exhaling bits of thin clouds of smoke. I mean it wasn't really what I wanted but I could definitely use it.

"Dis shit better not be no dirt!" I challenged right before I took a hit of my own. The shit hit my lungs like an attack from asthma. I let out a forced cough.

"Don't eva disrespect my shit, nigga. Dats dat straight gas." Fat laughed. I ignored his complacent remark, cleared my head from the dizziness, and took another hit of the earthly fuel. The smoke clouded my mind, making it hard to see through my thoughts. I needed that right now. Something to ease my mind. My eye sight was still pretty clear, even though I'm pretty sure they were low and probably red as hell. I just knew I was tripping when I was a 2017 Mercedes-Benz AMG 663 4 Matic pearl white SUV with carbon fiber trim. From the distance along with the heat waves it seemed as if the truck was floating in the mist of the air. It was like I was seeing a mirage, but I wasn't. "Dats big brah right der," Fat confirmed. "Jus' stay cool, Flex. Brah a lil' fucked up in da head. Fo' real

I think da nigga crazy, but he actually smart as a ma'fucka though!" Fat warned. Fucked up in the head? Crazy? Smart? I asked myself these questions through the clouds of my mind. I wondered what cloud possibly be worse than me? The closer the floating AMG came towards us, it was apparent to notice that the speed limit exceeded the average rate that one should be traveling amongst the loose gravel. This fool had to be doing about forty MPH leaving behind a grave trail of hazy dust as the tires kicked up rocks from its path.

The car came to a stop, damn near sliding on the paved gravel. The driver door swung open. Kayne West's 'Jesus Lord pt 2' was preaching through the audio system. The windows of the truck were slightly tinted. Light enough to see a silhouette, but dark enough not to see the details of who. The first thing I saw was the alligator pair of Stacey Adams as they landed on the ground. The man in gator footwear stepped from around the car door and slammed it shut. He sported a pair of dress slacks and a long sleeve all white button up dress shirt with suspenders over his shoulders fastened to his pants. He headed towards us with the confidence of a crocodile. The cockiness in his conduct was convincing. He stepped up on the porch and stood in front of us as if he was waiting on us to bow down in front of him or something. "De'Mon, dis better not be another one of dem games you like to play so much," he said.

"Come on now, big brah, you should kno' me well enough to kno' I ain't gone play wit no shit like dis," Fat replied. "Flex, dis our big brotha Slim." Slim was anything except that. He stood at about six foot and was definitely overweight for his height. Though I wouldn't exaggerate and say that he was extremely fat, but *slim* was an overstatement clearly.

"Pastor De'Angelo Anderson," Slim probably announced himself, extending a hand towards me. I was high as shit. Stuck. Fucked up in the head. I don't know if it was from the weed or from the fact that this nigga, which is supposed to be a brother of mine, just introduced hisself to me as a pastor. From lack of understanding I reluctantly extended my hand and embraced his. "I see you jus' like dis fool. You like blowing on dat shit." Slim stared into my eyes and then paused. I thought he was about to start preaching about how low and red my eyes were. "I can't believe you look jus' like my Pops." He stumbled the words out his mouth.

"Our Pops," Fat corrected Slim. "He ain't really believe a lot of da stories we heard." He directed towards me now as Slim and I released the grasp of our hand shake. "He always said dat it was blasphemy against Pops. Even though Pops told us out his own mouth, Slim didn't even think dat you and Q were real. He was in denial 'bout everything, even Pop's death. He still have dis prophecy of Pops havin' a second comin' like Jesus or some shit like dat. I told you dude was kind of fucked up in da head." *I guess that makes all of us*, I thought to myself. I've never felt so familiar around strangers. I couldn't deny the blood ties. Even with different mothers we all still looked overly favorably alike. Fat and Slim was actual identical twins but the three of us could possibly pass as triplets. Quadruplets, if Q was still here.

"I keep tellin' you, lil nigga, stop callin' me crazy." Slim approached Fat verbally.

"I ain't say you was crazy. I said dat you fucked up in da head." Fat defended his word.

"Same thing, demon, I mean De'Mon. Let me hit dat." Slim reached for the blunt, demanding instead of requesting. Fat handed it to him without protest. When Slim hit the blunt

I could definitely tell that it wasn't his first time. "Y'all heathens can't judge me. Nigga's got my head spinning wit all dis family feud foolishness." Upon exhaling God's green earth, I could sense the tension escaping from Slim's body. "So it's really true, huh?" Slim asked me what I knew of Pops. He wanted to know my version of our father. The part that he never saw. Fat was more curious about Q. I wanted to know why the fuck these two country fuckers got to live down here in abundant luxury while Q and I were tuck in the gutters of the city. It made me feel even more sorrowful at the fact that I was the one that stopped him from heading here. Looking back at the beginning of all this bullshit, I basically unintentionally handed my brother over to my true worst enemy. The law.

Fat, Slim, and I sat and caught up on the couple decades' worth of missing pieces of our lives. For the time being I had actually stood over the errors of my actions. The consequences to my choices. The trauma of my dramas. You know, like I really believed that things would be okay. As if I wasn't a dead man walking. I don't really do this much, but I could promise you that if I made it through this manifested hell on earth of mine, it'd be hard for you to convince me that God wasn't real. Not only was he real but also that he cared for the struggles of our sins. I already felt a change happening. I wasn't sure if it was as a result of being around these two niggas, the actual loss of Q, or the fact that I barely held on to my soul by a pinch of the finger tips. One thing I could say was that I felt right here. Right here on this porch with these two fools. It felt destined. As if all that I've been through in this life of mine, errors and all led me up to this moment. If what I felt was true, authentic, then that must have meant that there was a reason. A chance for change. Into what, though, I was completely unsure of. Who I am is all I knew how to be.

Damn near an hour and some change later, Lil' Shawty and Two came strutting out of the front door onto the front porch. Between the bonding with my brothers and blowing on this bomb weed, I was so high on cloud nine that I almost forgot about the two officers of the law who ran off with a fugitive. Lil' Shawty was squeezed into a black pair of leggings with the word *Dior* written in white letters rising up her left thigh. Her shirt was a tight white *Dior* shirt with black letters written across her breast. Her slippers were black *Dior's* with furry top straps, toes out, painted white. Her hair was wrapped around into a neatly tight bun. She even carried a bag that matched her linen.

Two exhibited a pair of daisy dukes shorts made by Chanel. The fabric of the denim was cut so short that the two front pockets of the shorts hung low, sticking from underneath the daisy dukes. Her shirt was a stylish blue and white plaid button up with the sleeves rolled up a little past her elbows, while the bottom of the shirt stopped just above her pierced belly button. Loosely tied in the front as if the shirt was made that way, the attire resembled the original style of the famous designer Co-Co herself. To top it off, Two wore her hair in two pigtails underneath a straw hat. She ended it with her bare feet in a pair of all white Air Force 1's. In addition to all of that, the large golden hoop earrings, gold bangle bracelets, and thin tennis ankle bracelet. Two was a mixture of a country cowgirl and a ghetto fabulous ratchet.

Both of the ladies were beautifully stunting to say the least. Even though I found Lil' Shawty sexy in her uniform, I rarely ever had the chance to see her in regular clothes. Besides, I liked her way better without nothing on at all. My brothers and I stared at the two beauties in awe. Yes, even the pastor admiring with lustful eyes. I couldn't blame him. Anything other than that may be questionable. After all, he was still a man and they were still shaped by the hands of God. Blessed.

"Why y'all lookin' like dat? Like y'all ain't ever seen a couple bad bitches befo'?" Two asked before blowing a bubble with her gun and popping it.

"Why you dressed like dat?" I asked in return. The question wasn't due to disapproval. I actually approved of her swag. I just wanted to irritate her flirtatiously.

"Cuz, dey say when in Rome, do as da Romans do. I thought dis would be a good throw off to my identity. Besides, it's hot ass hell out here already. It ain't even ten o'clock yet. Wat? You don't like it?"

"Now it's cool. Shidd—if you like it, I love it." Lil' Shawty was quiet. As I looked into her eyes I noticed there was a hint of jaundice there. To be honest, I loved that. For me, it only meant one thing.

Chapter Ten

Q

Tour of the Worlds

I was resting in my grave while contemplating a direction to push my plan into. So far, I was completely blank. Just a stream of empty space. While thinking of absolutely nothing, an angel had entered my grave, urging me to exit my grave. He said his name was Mike the angel of tours. Doing as I was requested, I floated to the surface of the earth. As soon as I was outside of the grave, the angel Mike snatched up my soul and rushed towards the sky. At that moment I had considered that I may have just made an irrational decision by trusting a demon who posed as a good angel. We thrust through the force field of the cemetery and accelerated higher into blackness of the night sky. We were so high that I had a bird's eye view of the earth. Within a tenth of a second we were above the clouds. There, a ride awaited our arrival. It was a chariot. Though not one resembling those of ancient times. The chariot was guided by two pale horses that spread wings amongst their backs like angels. I couldn't understand the purpose for the horses. The chariot was mechanical. An operation of machinery that was hands down way too advanced for this day in time. Another uncomprehensive aspect of this chariot was the two wheels. The chariot floated in midair unsupported from the wheels. At least that's what I assumed. The wheels weren't side by side the way I was usually used to seeing wheels. Instead, one wheel rotated inside another while the other revolved, creating a sort of equinox like meeting points at two different spots. Summarily, the spins and turns reminded me of the solar system minus the planets.

Sitting inside the roofless chariot was like riding in a spaceship. We skyrocketed higher into the sky at the speed of light. Although we traveled at lightning speed, phenomenally, everything around us seemed to move as if you was standing on the earth watching the clouds float by. Speaking of the earth, it was just about out of sight. From here it was the size of a tennis ball. That was until, without even stopping or slowing down, our direction of going up was rapidly reversed downward. As if the speed of light wasn't fast enough, now we traveled at the speed of darkness. I'm talking about so fast that everything went blank. Other than that chariot, horses and us, the only thing visible now was the swirling black hole that was directly ahead of us. Before I knew it, we were being vacuumed into the black hole.

Before I could actually set my sights on anything, I felt the heat. *Hell is hot*, is an understatement. Try *explosively scorching*, *volcanic boiling*, or maybe even *ferociously fiery*. It was a heat ignited by violence. A hateful heat that could melt the brain of a man for even thinking about it. Just entering the threshold of this place made me regret every wrong I've ever done during my lifetime on earth. I desperately hoped to be forgiven for every sin that has stained my soul.

Traveling now at a speed that was too slow for my liking, I watched as souls that have yet to enter the gates of hell scrimmage unsuccessfully, scrambling to set themselves free. There was a search for an exit but there wasn't any for them. They were dragged on the faces of their souls and thrown into the gate by the tens. Like every seven seconds the gates were opening, entering another load of souls. It was a chaotic crowd of chastisement. The sad part is that they weren't even in hell yet. It was like waiting outside the club. Except this wasn't that type of party. As more souls were thrown into hell, the almost equal amount was dropping from what seemed like an imperceptible ceiling. I concluded that with this systematic flow, the gates of hell was always busy. It wasn't even judgment day yet. Which made me wonder, are there any good people on earth?

"This is only the seventh level of hell," the angel of tours Mike said.

"Huh?" I foolishly asked, fully comprehending exactly what the angel said. It was the calculations that stunned me. "You mean there's more?"

"Yes. There are seven levels to hell. This is the one of least punishment. The deeper you go down the worst it gets. It's so much hotter just on the sixth level of hell that you wouldn't even be able to stand a visit." Hovering above the flames of hell, we scrolled over the gates. "It's surrounded with a force field here as well. Just like the graveyards." While listening to Angel Mike, I took in the visions of hell almost feeling the pains of the burning souls myself. One soul had a gun to his head in abominable tears. He pulled the trigger, using the spark from the gun to add to the flames of hell. His head exploded and his soul vanished. In vanity, his soul was replaced in the very same spot, in the exact same situation, doing the very same thing. "Since he's been here, he killed himself ten million, one hundred twenty-three thousand, six hundred sixty-five times. Six hundred sixty-six—In counting. Every time he does that, he feels the same pain as if it was the first time." I saw another soul continuously banging its head on an immovable stone. "That man has to live with the thoughts of his sins. They are so horrible that he attempts to beat them out of his head." Looking around, it was well over a hundred ways to die. However, they were all for no reason. Because however they die, they just seemed to reappear. Even worse than the repetition of the ongoing death was the ones that couldn't die. Instead, they were forced to endure the agonized pains of their sins. The leaders and followers alike pointed the blame towards each other for driving and guiding them to the hell fire. The disunity only worsens the outcome.

Steady moving above the flames, we continued to travel. I wasn't sure how long my poor little soul would be able to last here just on a visit alone. It seemed as if my soul was thinning from the beat, vaporizing me gracefully. I found some hope. Not for me, though, but for the souls forced to dwell here. It was a certain section for souls that were the company of angels to vouch for their loved ones, having the mercy from God to pull them out of the fires. "For the most part, these souls still feel as if they'd just spent an eternity in hell. And for a lot of the others, they will," Angel Mike assured me.

Finally, we were exiting the realms of hell through another black hole. I was starting to realize that these black holes were portals allowing travels between different spheres. The same torment of collected wind spinning so fast that it created its own space. Just like that we appeared back to the center of the universe. Once again at the speed of light we zoomed past earth. I took in every detail of our solar system. It amazed me. I was also relieved to be out of the dimension of hell. Just to be in this open space made me feel heavenly. Seeing just how real and terrifying hell was, I definitely felt the need to warn Flex the best way I could. Only thing was how?

Mike flew the chariot into the galaxy of the milky way. "This is the actual place where the souls are made, destined, and sent down to earth to live out their purpose," he said. "Here is where all souls shall return as well right before ascending for their judgment. A lot of souls may even get the chance to live out another lifetime before the end of time approaches." The chariot traveled through multiple places in the universe and the angel explained its purpose. For the first time I realized that everything mattered. Everything that appeared real, wasn't. And everything that didn't, was. Like thoughts, for instance. There was actually a place where every thought of the minds traveled to be transformed into a physical matter. It was crazy but true. I'm seeing it happen right now.

We reached the entrance of another portal where hundreds of thousands of souls ceaselessly floated up into a circular motion. Before we entered into a black hole, a fat giant snake that was big enough to pass as a dragon, flew towards us. A dragon with wings. It said nothing. Didn't even stop. It just zoomed past us trying to throw us off our path. The chariot was shaken from the turbulence. But right after we regained balance, we zoomed into the eye of the black hole. No matter how many times I went through these things, I don't think I could ever get used to the ride. The collection of souls, however, seemed to be in a state of full submission. They looked as calm as could be, twirling in the midst of the chaotic whirlwinds. It seemed as if in literally no time, we all were being squeezed through the eye of the dark portal. On impact the vision filled my soul with immediate joy. Everything glowed with illumination. A world of radiance, colorful creation, and love. All smiles. The only cries that could be heard was that of joy. Laughter and pleasant comments could be heard as we passed by. Hands down this was heaven. Thousands of angels flocked around working endlessly to serve our Lord. All was good. All of the worst fears were eliminated here. Worries were turned into bliss. The entire place was one way above any description attempted. To say it at best, you would have to see it for yourself. All I could promise you is that this was definitely the place to be.

After the tour was over, I was dropped back off into my grave. I was full of hope knowing that I actually had a good chance of making it into the gates of heaven. It also made me think more of Flex. Was it really worth risking heaven and falling into the depths of hell attempting to save him? What if I tried and failed? Leaving both of us to suffer the blaze of hell. Still fighting amongst each other. Blaming one another like I'd seen a lot of the burning souls in hell do. I laid back in my casket and considered my options. The first thing that came to mind upon my meditation was why I cared so much in the first place? Right before I was murdered, I had premeditated on a way to kill Flex. I was so sick from the pains that he had caused that it placed a piece of hate in my heart. The hate turned into depression. That depression clouded my mind with evil thoughts that eventually transformed into my actions. Now here I was willingly ready to put it all on the line for him. Sad to say that it may be a bit too late for a change of hearts. I always loved my brother. The type of love a dog had for its bone. If I could have, I would have kept him with me every step of the way. Thing is, though, that we all had minds of our own. We all had free will to make our own decisions. If I would have known that it would come to this, I would have loved him unconditionally regardless of his faults. I know the only thing that cured hate was love. Something in the gut of my soul was telling me that I had to take this chance. I had to make a move, and soon. Even if it killed me a fourth time. I stopped fearing death a long time ago.

Chapter Eleven

Flex

Bad Habits

Fat had received a call from his phone that urged him to move. Slim declared that he needed to head over to his church to handle some business of his own as well. You should already know that Lil' Shawty, Two, and I jump back in the F-250 with Fat. Next thing I knew—we were pulling up to another apartment complex which could definitely be considered as a project. Two projects in the middle of the country. That was two more than what I actually expected it to be.

Fat parked in front of the rental office. "Hold on right quick," he said before hopping out the truck, leaving the three of us sitting there.

"We need to be comin' up wit some type of plan to leave, Flex," Lil' Shawty said from the back seat.

"I am," I lied. Even though I knew she was right, I wasn't seeing anything wrong with this little spot. It actually wasn't as bad as I thought it would be. I was already scoping away to set up some type of shop in one or both of these miniature project spots. Learning from the mistakes of my past, I would definitely be smart enough to put together an escape plan.

"And we need to get rid of dat car ASAP," Lil' Shawty persisted.

"I kno' dat!" I grew slightly irritated but tried to swallow it down by focusing my attention elsewhere. A trio of niggas came out of an end apartment, stepped on the porch, and stood there. Four kids were busy playing on a playground nearby until they ran up to the porch where the group of three stood. The body language of the children was *overly excited*. One nigga who carried the confidence of a leader dug into his pocket and pulled something out. It was hard to see what it was from this distance. But the way he passed it to the kids, causing them to grow even more excited, I figured it was money. He whispered something in the tallest kid's ear. Afterward they all ran off down to the other end of the complex, rushing into an apartment. Maybe I was just tripping. But something didn't seem right. I don't know why but I definitely had that feeling. Now that I wasn't tripping about. I knew that feeling when I felt it. The only thing I didn't know was why.

"I'm jus' sayin', Flex," Lil' Shawty still yapped, not picking up on my vibration. I kno' you, Flex. You like to get comfortable, thinking you run shit and shit like dat. I've been watchin' you since we got here. Yo' eyes been lit up like a kid in the candy shop." I was easing the pistol from my pants as subtle as possible. I had long ago removed the silencer from the muzzle of the Glock. Shit made it hard to tuck the tool. The Glock rested in my lap now. The silencer was right in front of me in the glove department. I wanted to get it but didn't want the two in the back seat or the three on the porch to notice. I was reaching. "Flex! I kno' you hear me?" Now she was getting irritated as if I was the one nagging her. I nodded yes, but kept my focus on the porch.

Now I thought that I was tripping again. That was unusual because I never gave myself a chance to second guess. Anyway, I could have sworn that them niggas was watching me watch them. Knew I was right when the leader of the other two tried to inconspicuously point toward the truck. I caught it though. I was just unsure if he had caught on to my suspicion from the distance through the clean clear window or if it was just the truck itself that had their attention. Either way it went, was wrong with me.

"Flex!" Lil' Shawty raised her voice. It took everything in me not to turn around and shoot this bitch in the face. If my soul said to do so, I wouldn't be able to stop it. My killer's instinct had kicked in about a few minutes ago. "Boy, wat da fuck is—" Lil' Shawty had leaned up to the front of the seat, looking over my shoulder. "Wat da heck is you doin'?" She had obviously switched up her question. The gun was now sitting in my lap. Using her eyes to find the answer to her own question, she shifted her attention to the objects that I concentrated on. Without saying another word, she sat back into the back seat. A quick second later I heard a zipper zipping.

"Wat's wrong?" Two asked, snapping her gum.

"I don't kno', girl. Dis nigga on some." That's all she needed to hear as Two was next to rummage through her designer bag. I heard both of them cock their pistols and awaited whatever was next to come. The head nigga in charge of the three amigos stepped off the porch and the other two was more than willing to follow. "Wat da fuck dey ready come ova here fo'?" Lil' Shawty questioned. I was glad to know that she was focused now. For some reason the porch boys stopped dead in their tracks, after only taking a few steps. They looked past the truck; I followed their gaze. Fat was finally exiting the doors of the rental office. They stared at Fat from across the way in a state of confusion. Fat carried an all-black duffel bag in his right hand.

"Dey tryin' to rob him," was the conclusion, I spoke in a low tone of voice.

"Fo' wat though?" Two asked the question that we all wanted to know.

"Ion kno'," Lil' Shawty replied. "Guess we 'bout to find out."

Fat jumped back into the truck just as mirthfully as ever. He seemed as if he ain't have a care in the world. He tossed the bag over to me.

"Hold dis right quick, brah," he said. I immediately looked into the bag. It contained six pounds of weed. I already knew that before I opened the bag. My nose had told me so. The gas was potent loudly. I just wanted to know how much. "Dis da biggest order dis nigga eva put in," Fat said. "I was wondering when da nigga was gone level up. Nigga been coppin' a QP fo' da longest. Actin' like he was gettin' money. I see wats goin' on now. It was one of the oldest tricks in the book. Rocking the dealer to sleep. A consistent customer of low quantity all of a sudden copping big. Their movements, the play, the set-up, the whole vibe screamed robbery. All I thought of was murder. For one, anybody that robbed a nigga that was with me was an idiot. Two, I had already lost one brother due to the trait of disloyalty. Even though I didn't know this one as well, I would protect him as if I had nothing to lose.

Fat pressed his foot on the brake pedal, put the truck in reverse, and turned the music that was already playing up a little more. I turned it back down immediately. "Fuck you doin', niggaz?" Fat asked harmlessly.

"I need to hear myself think right now, brah." He looked me in the eyes for a quick moment. I knew he read my demeanor.

"Listen, brah," he still said though, "I kno' you gon' through more than wat I kno' 'bout, but you gone have to relax a lil'. Everything cool 'round des parts." I heard him but didn't reply. Were all my big brothers naive to the dangers of the world? Did they really think that love could overpower the evils of man? It irks me to see how green Fat was in this moment, while I was able to peep the shit out in less than a span of five minutes. Guess you couldn't see the picture when you stuck in the frame.

Backing out the parking space, Fat headed over towards the apartment where the men stood. "Damn des niggas out here already." He noticed for the first time. "Niggas thirsty as hell." *Yeah, they were thirsty alright,* I thought to myself. *Like wolves running through the woods.* And his ass was like a lake of water. Fat pulled up and parked. The men looked disappointed that he brought company. Fat went to grab the bag, but I held it tight. "Give me da bag, fool." he softly demanded.

"I'm goin' in wit you," I felt the need to say.

"Wat? Des niggas ain't on shit." Fat waited for a response. I said nothing verbally while saying a lot with my silence. "A'ight, man." Fat gave in. "You better not try to rob des nigga or no crazy shit." He was starting to climb out of the truck. This nigga was accusing me of something I was trying to prevent from happening. Guess it never pays to be me.

Before I opened the passenger door, I retucked the pistol. "We comin' wit you," Lil' Shawty told me.

"I kno'," I replied, stepping out the truck with the bag in hand.

"Mack! Wats up, nigga?" Fat approached the leader as if he was happy to see him. If he wasn't, he sure did play it off like a Will Smith. Fat came around the front end of the truck from the driver's side. I met him from the other side. Two followed me, hopping straight out the truck, bag in hand. Lil' Shawty followed up, walking around the back of the truck.

"Damn, Fat, you brought a bouncer and strippers too. Wat we 'bout to do? Throw a party at ten o'clock in da mornin'?" Mack joked and of course his flunkies laughed as well.

"He ain't no bouncer," Fat defended.

"So wat da fuck is he? Personal security or some?"

"Hell naw!" I could tell that Fat felt slightly offended by that last sly question." And dey ain't strippers." He cleared up before seeming unsure, cutting an eye towards the two dime pieces. "Ion think." Two popped a bubble from her gum but that was all that was said from the two.

"Maine, niggas tryna do business or wat?" I asked Fat only.

"Yeah." He spoke for the supposed to be customers. "So wats up, Mack? Wat we doin'? You gone invite niggas in or naw?"

'Oh shidd, I thought we was gone move like always fo' real. You kno', hop in dat truck flip flop and cop," Mack assumed.

"Naw, maine. Dats fo' dem broke niggas. You done bossed up now. You deserve a sit-down."

"Oh, so wat? You callin' me broke?" Mack made light of the comment.

"Not no more. I can't." Fat returned the humor.

Moments later we were inside the apartment. Fat and I sat on a couch across from Mack and whoever the other dude was. The third of the three remained standing, so Lil' Shawty and Two did as well.

"So wat you got, Fat?" Mack asked.

"Wat you ordered," Fat replied. For the most part I remained focused. But every now and then my gaze was lowered to the lines of power cocaine that was laid out on the table that sat in between us.

"To keep it one-hundred wit you, Fat, I was hopin' dat you could hit a nigga off wit a front." Now he was either stalling or trying towing it towards a plan b. Guess the extra company fucked up his party plans.

"You told me you had da money, brah. Wat type of games you playin' wit a nigga?" Finally, Lil Shawty and Two was catching on. Honestly though, if I wasn't here, it would have been way past too late.

"You want some?" Mack said, directing his question towards me. I lifted my eyes back up to him but remained silent. "I seen you lookin' a few times already. Go 'head and get you a line." I had the gut feelings of a genius. I mean I could tell within the first sixty seconds if I would prefer to deal with a person or not. I had a strong feeling that I would kill this nigga. I wanted to go ahead and get this shit out the way now. Being patient always gave me anxiety.

"He don't want none fo dat shit." Fat spoke up for me. He was wrong in a sense. My stomach has been turning and bubbling since yesterday. I felt a slight fatigue within my energy. A tightness in my muscles. Even my head ached for the shit. And as bad as I was trying to do something new and remain calm, the absence of the drug had my attitude highly present. Fat was right, though: I ain't want shit from this nigga.

"Aww, come on," Mack said, leaning down, taking a line up through his nostril. "It's all good. Everything straight. We all people here." He did a bad job at trying to convince me.

"Now, I'm good." I made sure he understood. Mack looked towards me in disgust as if my reflection made him sick. I could tell from the jump that he was pissed just by me being here. Now that he could see that I wasn't the foolish type to fall for childish games, it pissed him off more. I was starting to assume that this nigga ain't even have the money to pay just in case shit backfired the way they did. That meant two things in my world. This nigga Mack was a cold dummy, a rookie, and that Fat was sweet lick, an easy victim. Mack was running out of options. That's why he tried to use my weakness to pull me in. He was like a cat backed up into the corner surrounded by dogs. It was only one thing left for that cat to do: Scratch its way out.

I glanced over to my left. Lil' Shawty had her eye on my every move while keeping the standing man in her peripheral vision. The man standing and Two was having a staring match. His was sexual. Hers was more sanguinary. Guess when breaking the ice on that first kill, you became thirsty for the blood. I caught eye contact with Lil' Shawty for a quick two seconds before I turned back toward Mack. I think she knew. She was a fast learner. I snatched the pistol from off of my hip and laid it in my lap. These niggas was lacking, I guess not expecting this to happen. There wasn't a pistol in sight. The nigga standing tried a quick attempt to go for his gun but Lil' Shawty and Two was already on one. They both had their pistols in hand raised at the men. "I would suggest you don't do dat," Lil' Shawty advised. Put yo' fuckin' hands up. Get da gun off him!" she demanded towards Two. Seeing these bitches work, taking charge the way, they did, made me horny for murder. Two removed the gun from the man's waist. "Now sit da fuck down!" Lil' Shawty gave her next of orders. The man that once stood was now squeezing on the end of the couch besides Mack and his other partner.

"Hold up, hold up!" Mack said as if he wanted to shout but was wise enough not to. "Wat da fuck is dis? Wat y'all got goin'? Dis wat we on?" His hands was in the air, expressing submission. But he refused to control his tongue from blabbering on with a handful of questions. "Wat you call yo'self settin' me up for! Dats crazy. I see you on all bullshit, huh?"

"I aint—"

"Shut da fuck up, nigga!" I spilled through clenched teeth, scowling towards Mack, while at the same time shutting Fat up. "Stop actin' like you don't kno' wat da fuck gon' on or maybe you don't. Maybe you don't. Maybe you thought dis shit would be a piece of cake. A walk in da park. Like takin' candy from a baby."

"Wat da fuck is you talkin' 'bout, dude?" Mack asked, actin' as if he was a man of innocence. I told you once before that I knew a snake when I see one. This nigga was definitely a snake. Just not poisonous and small in its breed, like a garden snake.

"Put yo' fuckin' hands down, stupid. Da party's ova. And I swear if you ask one more fuckin' question, I'ma let dis Glock talk. Fo' now shut yo' mouth, open yo' ears, and maybe you'll find da answers to yo' questions. First of all, as you can see, my gun is in my lap so my warnin' in advance is dis, da moment I have to lift a finger to raise dis pistol dis bitch goin' off. At dis range, I can bet dat I could kill all y'all in four seconds. And dem two." I nodded towards Lil' Shawty and Two. "And divide dat number by three, y'all niggas a be dead in least dan one point three seconds."

I paused, glaring at Mack before going on: "Second of all, I hate to be lied too. So you can cut da act. I respect da code and I'll die 'bout it so I ain't tellin' you to expose yo' self. But don't play me like I'ma dumb ass. I been on you from da get go. Da plot was cool and you probably woulda gotten away wit it, if it wasn't for me. Oh yeah, fo'give me for not properly introducing myself. My name is—Satan." I was tripping in my head with laughter. You should have seen the looks on their faces. Them niggas was spooked. I had their ass ready to repent for all their sins. "Dat's right, y'all niggas done seen da devil in the flesh. Don't eva say dat I neva blessed you wit my presence. Now dis is wat's goin' to happen. Y'all niggas gone give my people his bread. I'ma hand ova dis bag, and we gone get da fuck out here. But remember, no games. And once we leave dis ma'fucka, y'all niggas better not even think 'bout layin' a hair on dis nigga." I pointed to Fat. "Trust me when I say I'm da devil. I bring da heat and I love da fire. Whereeva da smokers at, I'm der. I'll be der when it sparks and I'll be der when it clears, understood?"

"Yeah, maine, I got you," Mack said like a scared child agreeing just to duck an ass whipping.

"Okay. So da money, where it's at? No names."

The whole room was quiet for a long minute. Every second that passed ticked me off more and more. I hated waiting. Eventually Mack admitted. "I don't have it man." His voice damn near came to a treble pitch. I've never known a snake that squeaked. "Please don't kill me." He pleaded. I hated that too. Once my mind was made up to take a nigga life, nothing could stop me. No pleading in the world could. I respect those more who went out like a true soldier.

"Okay." I stood with the gun in my right hand. Bag in my left. "Now dat da cat's outta da bag, dis how we gone play dis hand out. We gone give you a lil' hand out. A seven-day trial." I laid the bag in Fat's lap who was absorbed with the intimidation I pressed upon Mack. Reaching into the bag, I pulled out two pounds one by one and dropping them on the table. "We gone start you off wit two fo' now. Next week when we pull up you need to make sure you have our forty-two hundred dollars. Nothing missin'. Ready fo' pick up." I got dat part of the grind from Q. "If you don't have dat mula it a be like sellin' yo' soul. So I suggest you hustle up. Fat, go get da car ready. Y'all go wit' 'em". I directed to Lil' Shawty and Two. "I got dis." They all did as I said.

I waited until Fat and the girls were out of the apartment. "You kno', today is a lucky day fo' y'all niggas. If y'all niggas don't believe in God, I think dat y'all should start prayin' askin' fo' forgiveness and apologizing. Cuz he is da only thing dat can save y'all right now. Da presence of da Lord is definitely here. Now I'm out dis bitch. But hear me clearly. If you eva try Fat in any mischievous intent again, I'll chop yo' head off and let da kids play soccer wit dat bitch." I paused and looked for a reaction. Them niggas was damn near scared to breathe. Just how I liked it. "And yeah. I think I would take some of dis befo' I go." I leaned over the table and snatched up a sandwich bag of the powder cocaine.

I backed out of the apartment all the way to the truck. As I thought, them niggas ain't even attempt to come to the door. While rolling out of the apartment complex, I dipped my finger nail inside of the sandwich bag, raised it and took a sniff up my right nose. I repeated with my left. I took a deep breath and relaxed my head back on the head rest. The drug sped my heart up some while slowing my thoughts down. This has been the longest twenty-four hours on the clock ever. "He think he Scarface," Two said, followed by a chuckle. I ignored her comment. No one else said a word. That's what I needed. A moment of silence. I don't think no one understood what I was going through right now. Shit, I didn't even know. All I knew is that I was tired. I wanted change but didn't know where to start. Why was I created to be this? I thought we were the masters of our own destiny? Was I destined for hell then? Was there another way for a project baby? An enforcer? I was starting to think Q was my way out. But the time on his clock ticked out. Now I felt like I was out of options. For the second time in tens of years, I dropped a second tear.

Chapter Twelve

Q

Searching for Hell

The way I see it, there were only two ways out of this grave-yard. Well, three, but I definitely didn't want to wait until this body decayed. The other two ways were by a chaperone, be either an angel or a demon. On the one hand, whenever an angel acted as a convoy, they was going strictly by the book. Obedient, breaking no laws. The demons, on the other hand, were all about breaking rules. I figured that if I could play their game just as good as them, if not better, then I could use them to take me wherever I needed to be. After seeing those other worlds, I knew that just the thought was risky. My mind was made up to take that risk. This is just what my soul was built to do: use the best of myself to bring out the better in others. I wasn't trying to be laying in a casket when there were better things to be doing.

I swished from beneath the ground and scanned the field. Burga was sitting on his tombstone enjoying a visit from a few of his homeboys. Spurting towards Stan's grave, I came across the soul I once overheard negotiating with a demon. I stopped at his grave. He looked at me like I was trespassing. "Wats up, nigga?" he asked aggressively.

I looked left and then right. "Man, I'm trying to get out of here." I tried to sound as convincing as possible.

The soul's frown turned into a smirk. "Maine, get da fuck out of here wit dat shit, nigga. Yo' ass can't even curse. Proper talkin' ass nigga."

"Naw, for real though, I need to get out of here. It's boring and blowing me out of my mind."

"Ain't dis a bitch! Nigga, you kno' you destined fo' heaven wheneva yo' number get called out of dis graveyard, right? And you mean you 'ready give dat up fo' wat?"

"Go to heaven for what? To be restrained within rules. I know the demons got it lit on earth. I'm trying to go dance with them. Get lost in the world. Besides, why do you care? You know how many stripes you'll get from the demons for swooping a soul like me out?" He made a contemplative facial expression.

"You kno' wat?" the soul stated matter-of-factly. "You right. Come back through here after sunset. I might have a way fo' you."

"Alright, bet." I agreed and started to travel off before I thought that through, and it made me stop immediately. "Hold up." I required the attention from the lost soul. "How come you still here stuck in the graveyard? Like can't you be out and about in the world?"

"Yeah, jus' not right now. I'm on recruiting right now, you feel me? Dis da best place fo' recruitin'. Don't trip though, fool, I'ma get you here. Remember, sunset, here."

Finally reaching my destination at Stan's grave, I knocked on his head stone. He peeped his head above the hole of his grave. "Q, what's up? You make it to the tour yet?" he asked, fully floating out of the grave.

"Yeah, I went."

"How was it?' Did it change your mind? I hope it did."

"It was everything you said it was. But no. It didn't much change my mind. Actually, it confirmed it. You seen that hell?" My tempo in the conversation grew with excitement as I thought back to the tour. "I can't let Flex blindly subject himself to those eternal conditions."

Stan starred at me as if he had pitted the fool. "So you mean to tell me that you seen all that, even the abundance of glory that the heavens have to offer, and you still want to risk it. You way more hard-headed than what I actually thought. Now I'm thinking I'm the fool for giving you too much credit. You know that there's a big chance that you'll end up in the same place that you trying to save Flex from, hell?"

"Yeah, brah, I'm aware of what I'm doing. I—"

"Listen, Q, I ain't leaving this spot until God gives me the OK to make the next transition. I got a certified ticket into heaven and I ain't messing that up for nothing or anyone in this world."

"No. Stan, I just came to let you know that I was about to go and just to ask two possibly last favors from you. If you can just keep an eye on my grave for me. At least until you go, if I'm not back by then. And if I don't make it up the stairs with you, please ask God to have mercy on my soul."

"Q, for the last time, I do not think that you should do this. Matter of fact, I know you shouldn't, it's against everything God said that we should do." Stan was now yelling to the back of my ghost. I was already making my way through the field of the graveyard. Deep down inside I had that feeling. The one where I wanted to cry. Although I was depressed with feeling within my soul, I was missing my physical body to express the emotion. At this moment I was happy my body was buried. At least I wouldn't have to wear my emotions on my sleeve or keep them bottled up in the chest of my body. Instead, my energy flowed and interweaved with the ether of the universe.

"What's up with you, Q?" Burga asked as I passed his grave on the way to mine.

"Nothing," I answered truthfully. Actually, nothing was wrong right now at this moment. Everyone was right. It was just that I dreaded the fact that I was willingly about to ruin all of that around.

"I see you over there kicking it with that trap soul dude. What y'all was over there talking about?"

"Trap soul?" I asked, more confused at the title because other than that, I knew exactly who he was talking about.

"Yeah, trap soul. That's what they call him around here because that's what he does. He traps souls!" Burga confirmed. "I hope you not making any dealing with him, Q? Only one thing can come out of messing with dude."

"Listen, Burga. I appreciate the concern. I really do. But my mind is already made up to do what I feel like is already done anyway. It feels as if I'm being pulled towards something. Maybe this is the way things were actually meant to be. So on that note I'll respect it if you stop trying to prevent me from fulfilling my destiny. Besides, if it was you, I would have done the same thing. This is how I express my love."

"Q, you don't have to sacrifice yourself in order to express your love. I thought you was smarter than that, Q. Q! Q!" I entered my grave and rested my back on the casket and waited until the sun was ready to dip low behind the horizons of the earth. Burga was still talking but I easily ignored him. It may seem harsh from his point of view. But the least I could do was not involve him or anyone else for that matter into my sinful matters.

I was so lost into doing nothing that it was like I was lost in space. It felt as if a whole eternity had passed while seeming as if no time had actually passed at the same time. "Ayee." I heard a voice calling just about a whisper along with the sound of someone knocking on my tombstone. Curious, I poked my head out of the ground. It was Trap Soul.

"What's up, brah?" I asked, fully exposing myself.

"You ready?" he answered my question with another one.

"I've been waiting forever," I confirmed.

Trap Soul laughed lightly. "Come on, we gotta go ova to my spot. I gotta a way out fo' you. I followed Trap Soul over to the place where his body was planted into the ground. Along the travels, my ears caught the sounds of shrills and begging cries from the results of terrible tortured souls. "Don't trip off dat. Dis da scary hours. A lot of souls are being punished in their graves right now." We reached Trap Soul's grave. I noticed that he didn't even have a tombstone. Just a plate in the ground. "Wait right here. He should be on da way soon." We waited for soon, and then waited some more.

"Q!" I turned around to find Burga's soul floating by the support of the air. "Don't do this, brah, please!"

"Brah, I already told you what it was. You shouldn't be here right now. You need to go back to your grave befo—" *Poof!*

"Here I go." A spirit appeared out of thin air in the form of an Instagram model. "I hear dat someone has made a date with destiny." By now I knew how the game went. From the lascivious, fraudulent appearance, the delusive delectation, and benevolence, I was sure that this was a demon.

"Yep." Trap Soul spoke up. "I told you I had another one," he said proudly. "A good soul too."

"Ohhh," the beautiful demon replied. "Good guy going grave, huh?" she asked. Shit, I don't blame you, dis place is a dump. Nothing but a big waste field. Anyway, enough wit da small talk. You down to ride? All you have to do is say so. Just give da word in agreement."

"Yep, let's go," I mustered as bravely as I possibly could have at that moment.

"Bet! Dats my nigga," the demon said, actually excited as she wrapped her arm around me. "Jus' call me yo' bitch! Okay, daddy? Fo' now, I'm yours."

"Q! No!" Burga shouted.

"Go lay it down, Burga. I'm good, brah."

"No, you not. I can't let you do this to yourself."

"You can't stop me, brah. Dis my life." My new bitch and Trap Soul was looking back and forth from Burga and I as we debated.

"You know what?" Burga asked a question he answered for himself. "You right. So if you go I'm going with you." Before I could even get one syllable out of my mouth, my bitch was wrapping her other arm quickly around Burga. She poofed us out of the atmosphere of the earth, shooting us farther into the sky. And, as the saying goes, what goes up must come down. Though this wasn't due to the force of gravity. We hastened so fast toward the bottom that we tore through wind. Now traveling through a complete pitch-black darkness, we dropped.

"Hey, bitch!" a voice shouted out. She was just as sexy as bitch was, with some succulent lips. "Took you long enough, bitch!"

"Dats my hoe ass sista," Bitch whispered into my ear. "Don't let dat hoe suck yo' dick, dat hoe got super head. Hey, hoe!" Bitch yelled out, turning her attention towards her sister. "Wat da fuck you been up to since a bitch been gone?"

"Shit, girl, chillin' wit des dog ass niggas." She was literally sitting on the couch surrounded by three dogs. "I need some soul dick, bitch, I hope you brought me some back wit you."

"Ion kno' 'bout him." Bitch pushed Burga out of her arm. "But dis one is all me. So keep yo' hoe ass mouth off him." She embraced me tighter in her grip.

"Girl, you kno' I fuck anything," Hoe said, excitedly hopping off the couch. "Besides, Bitch, you trippin'. Dis nigga fine fine." She grabbed Burga by his arm. "Come on, sexy, I'ma show you some new tricks." Burga was hesitant to go, cutting his eyes towards me. Hoe dropped down to the floor and sucked his dick up in her mouth. Immediately, Burga closed his eyes, throwing his head back with a moan while Hoe slobbed and sucked him up.

"Well," Bitch said, "it's ova wit fo' him. Dat nigga gone be gone off da head. I done seen dat Hoe suck souls to hell. Come on, my nigga. Our one-night stand gone be a classy one." Bitch held my hand as she guided me through a dwelling that was as big as a mansion but as filthy and occupied as a trap house. This joint was like a club. There was a party in the kitchen. Music and cards playing. Smoke blowing. Bottles pouring. Orgies on the counter top where pussy was the food. Fights. So many fights, but no one cared. At a separate table of six a group played Russian roulette. Whenever the trigger was pulled and the gun didn't go off, the person would be pissed. Moving on, passing a bathroom I saw another orgy. A bigger one with cocaine sniffing, heroin shooting, exchanging pills and molly through the tongue. It was crazy. Something I've never seen before.

Bitch stopped at a closed door and busted through it. Inside there was the first demon I ever saw since being a freed soul. It was Pig. She was in bed with a snake, who had its tail all the way up Pig's ass while it slithered its tongue down her throat. "Oh hell naw! Y'all nasty bitches gotta get da fuck out of here. I got company!" Bitch demanded.

Pig looked up from her face down position. Her face went from being screwed to surprised. "How did you get him here?" she asked in a whine. "I saw him first, Bitch, he mine!" Pig squealed like the animal she was, jumping out of the bed, rushing towards us. Bitch ran up meeting her halfway. Either Pig had heart or she just ain't know that Bitch had hands. She beat the swine out Pig.

The snake slithered up on me, creeping up my merged legs, circling my body. It hissed into my ear. "Hey, handsome." Come to find out the snake was a she as well. "You wanna tangle?" she asked.

"Naw. I'm good." I said more out of fear than repugnance.

"Scaredy cat," the snake teased with the whip of her tongue just outside my ear. "Come on, Pig. Get yo' fat ass up, bitch. You kno' you can't fight. Let's go finish dis somewhere else." The fight stopped and Pig got up off the ground.

"Yeah, dats right. Y'all kno' who da top bitch is 'round here. Get yo' thin ass outta here! You and dat fat bitch. Lookin' like the number ten!" Bitch shouted.

The odd couple of the pig and snake was gone. Bitch slammed the door behind them, grabbed me and threw me on the bed. "Sorry 'bout dat, daddy. I didn't mean to keep you waitin'. Des bitches could be very disrespectful 'round here at times." She slammed me on the bed from my sitting position. She climbed on top of me and for the first time since my death I felt sexually aroused. She stuck a finger into my mouth. Taking her other hand, wrapping it around my throat. She straddled my saddle with her hips like an equestrian, applying pressure with the hand gripped around my neck. At the same time sticking two of her fingers deep inside my mouth. This bitch was super aggressive. To the point that it was almost scary. The hotter her temperature grew, the wetter her pussy dripped. In addition to that, her eyes were turning red as she turned up the aggression.

Bitch pounced away for what seemed like hours, though the time still was no factor. Bitch and I both exploded in multiple orgasms but that didn't matter either. She just kept going and going, not even asking me if I wanted to stop. Not even once. I tried to sit up once but the bitch overpowered me, pinning me down to the bed by my hands. I ain't gone lie to you, though, the pussy was fire. If it wasn't for me trying to focus on my mission, I wouldn't have wanted to stop. Bitch leaned down and stuck her tongue deep down my throat. It felt as if she was trying to suck the air out of my soul. She sucked my tongue into her mouth and bit down on it with her teeth. I felt the pain as if I wasn't out of my body. It caused her to laugh as she continued to roll her juice box over my straw.

"You like dis pussy, daddy?" Bitch asked seductively, hands still pinned to the bed. Tongue still numb from the pain, I said nothing. She laughed an evil laugh. "Don't worry. You'll get used to it. I'll have you turning ova in yo' grave in no time." Little did she know, I was already planning a way to trick her to take me back to earth. I wasn't trying to get stuck in the waiting room to hell. I just hoped that even at its beginning stage that I wasn't in too deep already. All I knew that it was all or nothing, and from here I was all in. There wasn't any turning around. I had to figure this shit out. Only thing was that I now had Burga with me. So I had to think for both of us.

Chapter Thirteen

Flex Takes Heed

As the wheels on Fat's truck continued to turn, he traveled from location to location. Some spots he picked up money. Some spots he dropped money off. Only on a few stops was used to distribute more weed. It was obvious that he was doing something more than weed. I just couldn't figure what it was. He showed no signs of dealing any other type of drugs whatsoever. From experience, there were a few occasions where I had to hit the city picking up a few dollars that niggas owed me but this was different. Way different.

Fat went back and forth to this one particular Wells Fargo bank. I'm not sure if this was the only bank in town or if this was his favorite one. What I did perceive directly was that he didn't need to use an ID. They certainly knew exactly who Mr. Anderson was. Most of the transactions were all deposits. No withdrawals. Although, on one happening, I watched as Fat wrote out a check and dropped it off to the office of a corporation. From the outside looking in, I wasn't sure if he was doing anything wrong or everything right. Whatever lane he was in would definitely require a GPS in order for me to travel in it.

Pulling back up at the family's house, Fat parked the truck and sparked a blunt. "How'd you kno' dat Mack was plannin' to rob me?" he asked after meditating on cloud nine for a while.

"Shit was see-through from da jump, lil' brah." Fat coughed for the first time though. I don't think that it was caused by the smoke. He eyed me a little funny until I understood why. "I mean big brah," I corrected myself this time before continuing. "I got a keen eye fo' shit like dat fo' real."

"Dat's how I kno' all dis shit is being moved by fate," Fat said, inhaling deeply while passing the blunt to the right.

"Wat you mean?" I simply questioned.

"Cuz," he said. "You was meant to be here. Imagine if you weren't and I would have gone to make dat play walking into dat situation blind. A nigga like me would have been dead cuz I ain't give up shit fo' free. I had to work my way up to where I'm at. While niggas was blowin' dey money wasting time buyin' fun and fake love, I made sacrifices. Stacked my bread and invested it wisely." I pondered on Fat's remark for a moment. Just the phrase of him saying that I was meant to be here was confirmation to my own feelings. Other than that, in a world where nothing made sense, I just wanted it figured out.

"Can I ask you some?" I looked towards Fat, extending the blunt.

"You jus' did," he said, taking the blunt out of my hand. From the back seat of the truck. Lil' Shawty chuckled at the comment while Two giggled. Fat looked to the back seats. "Y'all don't smoke?" he asked, matter-of-factly offering the stick of weed.

"No," Lil' Shawty denied.

"It really wouldn't matta though, shit," Two replied. "Y'all got us suffocating back dis bitch." She attempted her best to fan away the smoke clouds with her waving hand. Fat laughed.

"Now, I'm talkin' 'bout other den da question I jus' asked you." I spoke trying to retain his focus.

"I was just fuckin' wit you brah. Wats up though?"

"How do you have all dis shit? Cars, farm land, big house, a couple cabins, but you still live where you live? I mean ain't dat da fall of all hustlas, being trapped in our old environment? Stuck in da box?

Fat took a deep hit from the weed and exhaled slowly. The inhale was so strong that he damn near had no smoke to blow back out. It all stayed within his body to mingle amongst his lungs. Then he dropped the bomb. I own Westside Village. My wife and I. And dat other complex we pulled up too." It felt as if my jaw had dropped below my shoulders. I know I may have looked dumb in the face, but it was stuck that way. "All 123 units' apartments. Westside Village is almost four times bigger. See, Flex, I figured why not? I always knew dat I wanted to buy da neighborhood where I grew up at. Once I did, I thought it'd be best if I moved back in da apartment from my childhood. Not just to save tons of money, but also fo' motivational purposes as well. Livin' der reminds me dat I'm not where I want to be yet. It feeds my hunger, pushing my ambition. I'm not der because I have to be or because I have fear of movin' on. It's jus' all part of da plan, lil' brah." Fat looked over towards me and laughed at my facial expression. "Here, man." He handed the blunt over. "Dis shit a help you pick yo' face up."

Fat gave me a few moments to hit the blunt and let it all sink. I ain't gone cap. I never once even thought about buying Jackson Ward or any other property for that matter. Q mentioned it once, and thinking back to that conversation remind me of just how much in the way I actually was. "You looked surprised at wat I'm tellin' you, Flex." Fat continued. "You shouldn't though. Another thing you shouldn't do is underestimate yo'self or anyone else. You are very much capable of achieving wateva you decide to focus yo' mind on. If you focus on a whole bunch of bullshit, den you'll create da mastery of nonsense." My life itself was living proof of what Fat had just spoke in his last words. So much so that it made perfectly good sense. Almost too perfect. If Q never told you then I'll be the first to do so. I was one arrogant bastard. At one point in my life, which was not even that long ago, I wouldn't let a nigga tell me shit. Not a got damn thing. I wouldn't give a fuck who it was. I wouldn't even give a fuck if I was looking in the mirror. Hell, I wouldn't even take heed of words from God himself. At this moment though, I felt as if it was actually God who was speaking through the vessel of Fat. Which meant to me that the big man upstairs still had an eye on me pushing me slowly towards hope.

"A'ight, look, we got all day to kick it, but now it's time to put in some work," Fat said, reaching over to the glove department and literally pulling out a pair of gloves. He handed them to me. I know I was just talking all that God stuff. And I really meant it. But for real for real, I was always willing to put in some work. What can I say? The shit is just in me. What you expected for me to do, change overnight?"

"Shidd, one thing 'bout me, I'm always down. Wat we on?" After I asked the question I had realized that I spoke a little too soon.

"Gotta hit da field," Fat responded, opening the truck door. Gotta do some farmin'."

"Farmin'?" I asked.

"Yeah, nigga. Wat you think da vegetables gone cultivate dey self? Da garden is similar to da mind. If you don't tend to it, then it will grow wild. You have to invest time into pullin' up weeds and removin' anything harmful to it. Da mind, just like da soil, is fertile ground. Wateva you plant into it, dats wat it would bring forth. You like to eat good, right?"

"Yeah," I simply answered the obvious. "Who don't?"

"A'ight den. How do you think it's possible without hard work and genuine care?" I had no answer. "Come on. After today you gone have more respect fo' da farmers of dis world, da world itself, da food you eat, and more importantly yo'sef." He hopped out the truck. "Y'all two can go chill in da house if y'all want to. It's open or you could jus' sit out here it doesn't matta. My wife should be pullin' up soon. She likes to cook and help me out in da field sometimes. When she gets here, she will keep you company. Let's go, Flex."

I followed behind Fat. For a while I stood there watching him work as he continued to school me about the world I was lost in. Before I knew it, I was hands and knees in the dirt taking orders in the line of work. Soon my pride had begun to step to the side, allowing me to give my all to the task at hand. For hours on in Fat and I crawled up and down the paths of the field. I don't know if it was the weed mixed with the coke but I was super focused. I crept through the tall plants like a tiger in the jungle hunting for its prey. Fat put me on game about the hustle that got him here and where he planned to take it to. Every minute I spent around him I felt that I could trust him more and more. Always being the least trusted person, I wanted him to feel safe in my trust as well. I learned in these few hours that he was anything but green and that he was far from soft. He just did everything out of love. Which was something that I knew nothing about and was willing to learn from. The thing with me was that I always wanted to be the boss. Yet I never took the time to learn how to be that and was unwilling to put in the work for the status. What other way to start than from the ground!

When the work was finally over, I felt muscles that I've never flexed before. As we headed back towards the house, it was perfect timing when Fat's wife, Lil' Shawty, and Two stepped out onto the porch with two plates of food and glasses of lemonade. While we ate, Fat convinced me to start thinking long term while focusing on what was going on in the moment. He referred back to the garden. "When you plant a seed, you expect it to grow. But in da process, you continue to feed it. Give it water. Make sure it sees da light. And most importantly, put love into everything you do." He had me thinking harder than ever. Brung my awareness that my brain muscles is the one I should be flexing the most.

Chapter Fourteen

Q

Demon's on Da Saints

"Bitch!" Her sister yelled, busting through the door as I busted my tenth orgasm.

"Wat, hoe? Damn!" She answered after removing my ghostly penis from out of her mouth.

"We gotta get back to earth like now, Bitch! Niggas is gon' crazy up der right now. Bodies are droppin' and dey cute too."

Bitch jumped up from her knees and started to leave as if I wasn't even there. I grabbed her by the arm before she could travel out of my reach. She looked back at me as if she would kill me if I wasn't already dead. "Boy, wat da fuck is you doin'? Get da fuck off me!" she demanded.

"Oh now I'ma boy. I thought I was your nigga?" I attempted charm.

"You was my nigga," she replied in a cocksure sense. "It's ova now. Wat? You was expectin' to get married and shit? Boy, please, shit wasn't even dat good. Plus you could barely handle a bitch. Now let me da fuck go!"

"I don't care if you was everybody's bitch. I just want you to take me with you. I can help you. That's what I came here for." She sucked her teeth.

"How da hell is you gone help me?" she asked.

"I seen how when the souls exit the body. Most of them are confused. I could convince them to go with you easily. I can—"

"Look, wateva y'all ma'thafucka's gone do, y'all need to hurry da fuck up with it!" Hoe shouted, still standing in the doorway.

Bitch decided to let me slide with her. I even pleadingly persuaded Hoe to snatch up Burga. Tell her that it would be better with the more of us. Somehow, not to my surprise at all, we poofed into the streets of Jackson Ward. Right in the middle of a shoot-out in the middle of the projects on Saint John Street. A bullet flew through the heart of my soul. Though the pain wasn't physical, the heart of my soul ached from the vision.

After the oneness of unity that we had established, it came back full circle to this. Residents of the same neighborhood aiming at each other's heads with deadly weapons. Maliciously meaning to murder a man while only adding another malfunction towards their own soul. In a sense, only senseless killing themselves. I'd probably rather stayed in my grave than to set my sights on this image. Pistols popped. Bullets bullied bodies. Bodies fell. Souls were snatched or pulled out of the cages of their bodies. Being awaken to the awareness of the real world. Their existence destined for either heaven or hell. As expected, most souls were confused. Obvious that their thought was that death was the end to all. Surprised to find that it was just the beginning.

I continued to stand in the middle of the chaos. But this time if I spoke then my words wouldn't be heard until it was too late. Angel and demons battled over the souls. Souls became prisoners of war or either safe from the mischief of the evil ones I spotted Reggie and Lil' Mark, together, ducking and dodging. Not bullets though, but demons and angels the same. They laughed. It was funny to them like a joke of some kind. Though the fact that they refused to be captured was serious. "Reggie, Lil' Mark!" I screamed for their attention. Reggie swiftly snapped his head towards the sound of my voice.

"Oh shit!" he said, rushing over to me with Burga at my side. "I see you popped out jus' in time! Mosby and Da Ward beefin'. Des niggas got da nuts to hop out on feet and walk through dis bitch. Niggas lucky I ain't alive. I would have knocked like five heads off by now! "Reggie was overly excited about something that he had no control over. "I ain't gone cap though. I kno' he yo' brotha and all dat, but I'm lookin' fo' Flex. Dat nigga somewhere ducked off good. His bitch ass ain't popped out yet. Dat nigga usually be front line. Now all of a sudden, I can't find him."

"Flex is nowhere near here," Bitch said, pulling up to our conversation.

"Shut up, Bitch!" Reggie demanded of the slutty demon before asking her to speak again. "How da fuck you kno' dat anyway?"

"Flex is one of us. Jus' like you. We always keep tabs on our biggest fuck up's. Dat's where all da souls are being snatched up at."

"Reggie, you know this bitch?" I asked.

"Yeah, I kno' Bitch. Shawty fucked da shit out me den kicked my ass to da streets. I thought we was gone thug together and all dat but dat bitch fo' everybody." I silently agreed.

"Yep, I sure am." Bitch agreed verbally. "I see how y'all niggas be doin' dem bitches when y'all on earth. Won't get dis bitch."

"Shut up, bitch!" Reggie repeated this time with a little more anger. "Where da fuck Flex at?" he asked, giving her permission to talk again.

"Flex ass is somewhere in da country and dats all I'ma tell you." That's all she had to say for me to know exactly where he was. I wondered what made him want to go there. If any-thing, I hope he didn't travel that far distance just to mess someone else's life up.

"Why da fuck you ain't been tell me dat shit, bitch?" Reggie yelled.

"Cuz, dummy, yo' ass ain't ask." She snapped her neck while rolling her eyes.

"We gotta go find dat nigga,' Reggie said to Lil' Mark.

"I kno' where he at," I said truthfully, not knowing if that was a good or bad decision. I knew that Reggie's intent to find Flex was ill-willed but I had an idea to kill two birds with one stone. Well in this case, save two souls with one prayer. "But how we gone get to him without usin' demons?"

"We don't need dem bitches no more. We on earth again. Niggas jus' can't see us. As long as you don't let one of dem snatch you, you good. We can travel anywhere on earth, we want. But my question is, why da hell you out here lookin' fo' Flex and not in da graveyard wit yo' body?"

"I want to find a way to get him killed," I told a half lie to Reggie. I once read somewhere that a half-truth was a whole lie. But the truth is that I really did want to kill Flex, not the body of Flex or his soul, but the one third of him, his ego.

Reggie stared at me. Burga stared at Reggie, waiting on a reaction from him. Lil' Mark stared at Burga, trying to figure out why he stared at Reggie so hard. I waited for Reggie to buy into my bent-up truth. "Dats how you kno' when a nigga got real love fo' a nigga." Reggie started to express that ugly smile of his. "Nigga down to ride on his own brotha dat nigga too, huh?" Burga just hunched his shoulders nonchalantly, not really knowing what to say. "Shiddd, wat da fuck we waiting fo'?" Reggie asked. "Let's go hunt dis nigga down. Ain't shit happenin' out here, jus' niggas dyin'. Same shit every day.

Dem niggas gone be mad as a ma'fucka when dey soul get snatched and they see how real shit is." We headed off.

Chapter Fifteen

Flex Takes Lead

Three Months Later—

Within this ninety-day run I learned something valuable about myself. I was a fast and effective learner, when I fully concentrated on something. Every day of my last ninety, I spent two thirds of the day either working or learning a new trait. No days off. I used the same energy that I use to trap with and transmuted into my work effects. The thing about the work I did was that it was the best work of all. Working for myself. In my mind, it was so similar to trapping that it was basically the same. The biggest difference was that the money was consequence free, the work was productive, and it actually led me to a less stressful drama free life that I wouldn't mind living. Speaking of money, productivity, and living, in this business of mine they had something called estimated net worth. Let's just say that you brought a brick and plans to break it down however way you wanted to. Depending on what your prices would be expecting to make back. Same thing. Anyway, in the next nine months the business that I mainly focused on had an estimated net worth of 1.3 million dollars of course nothing was in my name. If you know the game, I wouldn't have to say that. Let's just say that Fat and I were under-the-table partners.

I'm pretty sure you're curious as to what type of business I had jumped into. Agriculture. But before you judge though, you should check my history. Certified street nigga and I'd shoot your teeth out one by one and see if you would want to laugh with an empty mouth. You know what? My bad, you know I have both anger and pride issues. Be patient with me while I work on them. Back to the business, though. Agriculture is in high demand right now with little supply. To coincide with supply and demand the location was perfect. It was as if that same brick that we spoke of earlier, you was the one person in your city with that drug of choice. Yeah, right, don't even picture it.

Keep up with me, though; I had food moving like train on the tracks. I used half of the money that Lil' Shawty and Two accumulated and invested—one hundred thousand—into my new playing field. I brought two hundred chickens, as my first animals, planted various vegetables and fruits that we didn't have at first, and expanded the produce by my own hands with the help from the others. That was three months ago; for the most part, it was all paying off.

Fat was happy about my push of determined ambition to say the least. He was more than ready and willing to assist me in any manner I see fit with the growth of business. On my first day of arrival, Fat had put me on game about his already established business which was the initial motivation for me to get on my business man suit. In addition to the two apartment complexes that he owned, he also owned a towing company along with a small dealership. As he advanced my aspects on the business, I helped him expand his hustle with his weed production. I suggest that he go legit with that as well. He humbly told me that now was not the time but it was soon to come once he ran down all the taxes that came with owning a weed dispensary. I agreed. How I did find purpose to pursue him into expanding out already legit business. I thought of a family grocery store where we could distribute our own foods. Even a trucking company so we could deliver the food ourselves as well. Now that my thoughts were flowing in the positive directions, my head stayed up in the clouds. But not on the usual arrogant type shit that was on. More like the sky was the limit. All I thought was big thoughts. No more small shit. Fat promised me that we would start on the goals I have in mind. Starting with the first step. Business plans.

Lil' Shawty and Two both wanted to do their part at helping me generate some Benjamin Franklins. They took the other half of the money we had and invested it in something that they both loved, clothes. With the universe bringing things together like a dove tail, just so happened Fat's wife was a skillful sewer. Together they made a promising team. I saw something that started as a hobby with the potentiality to be something great. They call it soignée. Speaking of Lil' Shawty, she was now about four months pregnant. I can't really say how I felt about the news. I was excited about the birth of my first seed. Truthfully, though, the reality of my life pained me to the core. No matter how fast you tried to, it was impossible to run from your past. Even though things were going good now, I knew that I would come a time where I would have to face the consequences of my old self. That's where the pains came in at. Not the part of taking responsibility of my actions. I would stand on them like the G that I am. It was just knowing that I may not be able to be here to raise my seed. I think that's another motivation that pushed me forward. Just in case I could physically be here for my child, I would make sure to leave something behind for them to grow with.

"You a'ight, baby daddy?" Lil' Shawty asked me coming from under the covers, crawling towards me. I sat on the edge of the bed blowing on a bag of that bomb weed that Fat produced with his own hands. I inhaled deeply for about five seconds, held it in for another three and exhaled it slowly for account of about ten seconds. I was reflecting on it all.

"You like callin' me dat, huh?" I asked nonchalantly.

"Yep. Sure do. Problem?" she replied with a hint of sarcasm.

"Don't act like you don't love it." She placed both of her hands on each side of my shoulders and softly but firmly massaged them. Leaning in closer, she passionately kissed me on the neck. "You kno' I love you, right, Flex," she whispered in my ear low before sticking her soft tongue around the rim of it. I knew it but didn't say it. Instead, I took another hit of the gas. "I'm so proud of how hard you've been working. And I want to show you just how much I appreciate you." From my back side she rubbed both of her hands past my chest, down my abs, and stopped at my belt buckle. Unfastening it, she now massaged my manhood. It didn't last too long, though. Before I knew it, she was heading off to the bathroom that was stationed in the bedroom, leaving my dick rock hard. "Hold on, wait a minute. I got a surprise fo' you." She returned within less than a minute, holding something in her hand that she hid behind her back. Climbing back onto the bed, she placed her body behind me. Next thing I knew—she was positioning her hands in front of my eyes with a bandana in her hand attempting to blindfold me. I grabbed her wrist with my free hand.

"Wat da fuck you think you doing?" I questioned as calmly and seriously as possible.

"Wat? You don't trust me?" she asked. I thought about it but didn't reply. "I got a surprise fo' you but you not gone get it unless you prove dat you trust me first." Like I said, you couldn't run from your past. If this was the day I had to take my fall, then fuck it. Slowly I released my grip on her wrist and hoped that it didn't result in a raid of police. "Aww, look at you," Lil' Shawty teased while wrapping the bandana around my head. "Somebody growing up. I promise you'll love dis." Then it got quiet.

I could feel Lil' Shawty getting off the bed. I thought about peeking. "Yo better not cheat, Flex, or I'm takin' it back." I heard the door open and Lil' Shawty's voice traveling down the hallway. I waited. After a couple more hits of the blunt, I heard footsteps followed by the door being closed. Right after, my dick was being gently removed from my pants and drawers. It was placed into a wet, warm, and mellow mouth. She generated a smooth motion, picking her head up and dropping it back down. She mixed in a few twists and turns. My dick head found the back of her throat and she ain't even gag. I moaned, though, I know she said she loved me but damn! Lil' Shawty never gave up the head like this.

Lil' Shawty removed the blunt from out of my hand. I'm glad she did because I damn near forgot that it was there. Common sense hit my complexity when I realized I had a hand on my thigh and another on my balls. So how the hell was she able to. The third hand grabbed one of my hands and I found it swimming in a puddle of wet pussy. I used my other hand to hurriedly peel the blindfold from off of my face. To my eyes surprise. I found Lil' Shawty sitting beside me to my left on the bed. With her legs wide open, I used a couple fingers to soothe her clitoris. She moaned softly as her juices soaked my hand.

I ain't have to look down to know who had my dick in their mouth. Though I surely needed confirmation, casting my sights downward, I was overly excited to see Two's jaws locked around my ego stick. It made it even more better at the fact that her eyes were waiting to lock in with mine. She sucked my dick like she had a point to prove. Like this was something that she couldn't wait to do all along. Like this was the last dick she would ever taste. It wasn't even my birthday but I felt reborn.

Standing to the side of me, Lil' Shawty who was laced in red lingerie stuck her tongue into my mouth while Two swiped her tongue over the length of my wood. Next, Lil' Shawty grabbed Two by her elbow, picking her up from her knees. Before standing up, Two took one more major slurp of the fluids caused by her sucking expertise. They faced each other. Their hands wandered around the curvy body frame of the other's. I watched for a moment, taking it all in. Pondering on the actions of the two bodies. Loving the vibe. I admired how Two's dark skin lustered through the blue sexual apparel that laced her body like the string of a shoe. A perfect fit. Her ass cheeks popped out of the thang where the palm of Lil' Shawty caressed the cuff of her rump. I love the way they sported the opposite yet corresponding colors of red and blue. Lil' Shawty being the fiery hot one while Two's blue resembled being cool and icy. Together they were a perfect balance and both aroused my sexual desire to it a high altitude.

Lil' Shawty led Two on top of the bed. Following her lead, Two bent over on all fours right beside Lil' Shawty. Busting it wide open, they both popped their pussy in a sensational like a set of strippers who had bills overdue. My emotional reaction enhanced my lustful desire drastically. I crawled behind the pair, approaching my own grown-up version of candy land. As an act of appreciation, I stuck my face in Lil' Shawty pussy. I waggled my tongue upon her pussy cat as if I was a thirsty dog drinking out of its bowl. Lil' Shawty whined and motioned her ass against my face while I ate from her cakes with my right hand. I played in the midst of Two's pussy lips while I used my left hand to spread the lips of Lil' Shawty in search of her clitoris with my wandering tongue.

Picking my face up, I lust more at the sight of Lil' Shawty and Two licking each other's tongue and planting kisses on the other's lips. I slapped Lil' Shawty's ass like the boss I was.

Being a boss, you got what you wanted, and what I really wanted was for my dick to be surrounded by the thickness of Two's chocolate and strawberry colored pussy. I rubbed my dick head at the entrance of her box. Just from that I could tell that it was a tight fit. I slowly eased in three inches and pulled it out. She moaned. I came back with five and pulled it out. She hissed like a cat from the pleasurable pain. Finally, I filled her up the whole eight-inch love stick. She jumped. "Don't run," I said, grabbing her hips, speeding up my thrust, fulfilling my desire of lust. Her head bobbed. Her hair bounced and her ass jiggled, always coming back to my pelvis area, making a clapping sound. She repeatedly screamed "yes!" Finding more comfort from the intercourse turning pain into passion. From there, the bacchanal was initiated. I got to keep it real with you though, this a whole lot of ass to focus on. So you gone have to get back with me later.

Chapter Sixteen

Q

Perfect Timing

Lil' Mark, Reggie, Burga, and I had finally reached our destination, blessing Flex with our invisible presence. Right now we were somewhat kind of eavesdropping in on a conversation that he held with a beautiful woman. The thing about the woman that triggered my unforgettable memory was that I had seen her before. It was only once but I remembered it as if it was just yesterday. I had dropped the mother of my son, Dawn, off at the campus of VCU before. While waiting for her in the car, this woman that was talking to Flex had walked by. Not only had she walked by, she also looked into the car staring me down as if she knew me. Right now, I was coming to the conclusion that maybe it was because despite our complexion and difference in eye color, that Flex and I barely favored each other. That was the biggest sense I could make out of our stare down.

"Will you just' tell me wats really botherin' you, Flex, please?" the woman who stood beside him asked with a hand laying on his shoulders as he sat on a bench that was positioned on a porch. "You keep sayin' dat you're good but I kno' dats not da truth. I kno' you been through a lot. You kno' you can trust me, at least you should at dis point. You have to talk 'bout yo' problems to someone. It's destructive to hold dem all in to yo'self. Now tell me, wats wrong?"

"Regret. Lil' Shawty. I'm livin' wit a lot of regret," Flex replied. I felt a wave of mixed emotions vibrating off his energy. The expression of his speech was different. It matured.

His demeanor was humbled. His pain was evident. Just at the confession of his regret was proof of his sorrow and remorse.

"Well, like I tell you all da time, Flex, yo' still livin' so ders still a chance to right all yo' wrongs. You can—"

"Now Lil' Shawty," Flex cut her sentence short. "You don't understand. It's some shit you can't take back. Things you can't undo. People you can't bring back." Flex leaned down resting his elbows on top of his knees, hanging his head down low.

"You don't have to beat around da bush wit me, Flex. I won't be able to give you my honest opinion if I don't truly know wat da hell you talkin' 'bout. Now stop talkin' at me and talk to me, please? So we can have a mature conversation." Flex lifted his head, exposing the few tears in his eyes and looked directly in the eyes of Lil' Shawty. "It's my niggas. And my brotha. I tried to kill my own brotha." He acknowledged one of his many already sins.

"Wat da fuck!" Lil' Mark and Reggie unified their question.

"He tried to kill you too, Q?" Burga asked, shocked. I just looked on.

"We need to find a way to kill his ass right now," Reggie suggested. "Dis nigga tried to take all of us out. Dat probably was his plan da whole time so he could come out here and live in dis big ass house wit dis big booty ass bitch." I silenced Reggie with a finger to my lips, shushing him.

Not just dat though. I knew Flex wasn't done. "I got da blood of my niggas on my hands," he said to the babe. He raised his palms up, staring at the inconspicuous blood that dripped down them. "Even though I didn't mean to, it's all my fuckin' fault. My attitude, lack of thinking and love had me in a hateful rage. Lil' Mark died by my side due to my misguidance. Dat young nigga looked up to me as if I was a king or some. But all I did was lead him to his grave at a young age.

"Burga got his point-blank range with a stray bullet. All because I tried to kill someone fo' speakin' truth. Burga tried to prevent it from happenin' but instead he put himself in harm's way. Still, it's all my fuckin' fault." He paused for a moment before going on:

"And Reggie. Damn Reggie." Flex buried his face in the palms of his hands, Lil' Shawty took a seat beside him wrapping her arm around his shoulders. "I did not kno' he was in dat fuckin' car. But even if he wasn't, it still wouldn't make it right. I only shot up da car cuz I thought it belonged to a bitch who dubbed me on da pussy. On top of dat, I was jealous like a lil' bitch becuz she had a car dat costed more than mine. Only to find out dat it was my brotha's car. Dat was my brotha's bitch. Da whole time, I jus' knew dat he was dead. Da fucked-up part is dat I didn't even give a fuck. Now dat he's really gone, all I'm left wit is regrets. All dat shit I did jus' to cover up being da blame fo' Q's death jus' to find out dat he wasn't dead da whole time. Ion think you could understand how fucked up dat left my already fucked up mind. Like where da fuck was he dat whole time?" So many questions left unanswered. So many whys left hanging in the air. I'm so unsure of what I'm sure of. It's almost feel as if Q was watching me at dis very moment." Lil' Mark, Reggie, Burga, and me all looked upon each other.

Lil' Shawty was left speechless. All she could do was lay Flex's head on the side of her breast and cradle him in her embrace. "You kno' my brotha hated to play da scene so he made himself an alias to match his presence. He called himself Ghost. I used to clown his ass. Told him he been watchin' too much TV. Sad to say though, and I hate to admit it, but he was right. Da whole time he was right 'bout it all. If only I had listened to him jus' one time."

"You can't sit right here and beat yo'self up 'bout it, Flex. It's good dat you feelin' bad 'bout yo' past dealings, and even better is dat you are gettin' it off yo' chest. But I'm pretty sure if yo' brotha could talk to you right now da last thing dat he would advise you to do was cry. He'd probably tell you to finish wat y'all started. Change fo' da best and reach fo' da heights of success. Look at wat you've done in three months. Imagine three years, or three decades fo' dat matter. Everything happens fo' a reason, remember dat. And God is da author of dis book. If you ask me, I'd say dat you was da chosen one. But it's all on you. You have to learn how to grow out of yo' pain. Take yo' dirt and make flowers. Hell, even roses have thorns.

Flex lifted his head and looked into the eyes of Lil' Shawty. "I fuckin' love you, Shawty," he expressed his self.

"I kno' you do. Yo' better, nigga. And you better kno' dat I love you back." They planted kisses on each other's lips before sharing tongues the French way.

"Maine, wat da fuck!" Reggie was obviously pissed. "You mean to tell me dat I got lumped on some humbug shit. After all dem continuous all night flight in a row on da block wit no rest, tryin' to get my money up. All dem cat naps I had to take wit one eye open. After all dem niggas dat tried, I get killed cuz a nigga thought I was somebody else? I can't believe dis shit. Da way he hit me up I could have sworn he was layin' on a nigga da whole time. Wat da fuck I'ma do now? I missed out on my own funeral jus' to make sure dis nigga Flex get killed. After hearing his side of da story, seeing him like dis, and knowin' dat he's shameful, I can't. But I don't even kno' where da fuck my grave at."

"No bullshit," Mark agreed.

"I been runnin' 'round wit des petty ass demons all fo' none!"

"Facts," Lil' Mark agreed with Reggie again.

"And den on top of dat shit—"

"Hold on, Reggie, I think I got a plan to get all of us back to our graves." I cut Reggie off, trying to ease him of his anxiety.

"Of course, you got a plan, Q. You always got a plan." Reggie was more sarcastic than anything. "I'm pretty sure you planned dis whole gathering' we havin' right now, huh?" Burga cut his eyes over at me. "Dis some bullshit."

Flex got a ring from his cell phone. He looked at the screen and was eager to answer it. "Yoo," he said in a voice as if everything was good. "Yeah, say no more. I'm ready to pull up now." Flex hung up the phone and looked towards Lil' Shawty. "Aye, boo, go get Two. We ready do fo' a ride right quick." She kissed Flex on the top of his head and did as he said.

The second woman who I considered to be Two came strutting out of the front door. She sported a perfect mix up of off white and Louis Vuitton from the top of her hat down to her red bottoms. On her wrist was a Cartier 18k white gold bracelet. Now that I realize it, Lil' Shawty was also covered in a couple famous designers. Her collaboration was Hermes and Fendi. Dripped with a Rolex day date 18k yellow gold watch. Seeing them caused me to pay more attention to what Flex had on. The thing that stood out the most was the Hublot wrapped around his left wrist. It was the big bang Mp-11 version covered in his favorite color, red. His top was a simple frosty white T-shirt. It had a YSL belt wrapped around his Balmain jeans and protected his feet with a pair of Prada cloud bust thunder sneakers. Red and black. I can't say what they were into but I could surely see that it was paying off well.

Flex got up and the two women followed him walking on both sides of him.

"Dis nigga got two bad bitches?" Reggie asked with a hint of envy.

"Come on, y'all. We gotta stay with Flex," I advised, completely ignoring Reggie's question.

"Fo' wat?" Reggie questioned. It's already fucked up enough dat I'm here fo' no reason. Now you tellin' me dat I gotta stay 'round dis nigga?"

"If we want to make it back to our graves this is the best way," I convinced the rest. "Wherever Flex is, the angels will eventually end up as well. Trust me." I followed behind what seemed to be a love triangle. My three accompanying souls followed behind me. Flex led us to a black-on-black 2020 Mansory Lamborghini Urus. Flex and his two climbed into the Lam truck while the four of us occupied the empty space.

We pulled up to a small apartment complex. Flex bumped a song called 'Quick to Judge' by Money Man. "Aye, fo' real though, shawty, I can't even hate," Reggie said over the music. My lil' nigga gettin' money out dis bitch."

Flex hopped out the car, music still blasting and all six of us followed. He pulled up on a group of niggas. Right off the back I could feel the tension in the air. Flex didn't even bother to dap any of them up. "Flex, wat's up?" The one who positioned himself as the main man greeted. He had a wicked smile sprawled across his face. The only person that I knew could match the coldness of the grin of a snake as good as this dude was Flex. "Sup, Mack? You ready on da bread?" Mack pulled out a stack of bills and passed it to Flex. He observed the money and without even counting said: "Dis shit feel a lil' short, fool. You kno' we don't do business like dat." Mack's grin grew.

"Yeah, it's a lil' short. Twenty-five hundred. But it's all der though."

Flex balled his face up and looked from the money in his hand back to Mack. "Da fuck you mean a lil' short. But it's all der?"

"Dats a fuckin' oxymoron. And I'm not wit da paradoxical shit. So I take it I must look stupid to you, huh?"

"Naw," Mack replied carelessly. "If I've learned anything 'bout you in des past few months it's dat you far from stupid. In fact, you are quite da intellectual. Therefore, you shouldn't find dis hard to comprehend. You see all of those lil' powder packs and favours I handed you, it came at a cost. Wat you thought."

"Oh, so you trying cut da ties of our business lose?" Flex interrupted.

"Naw, I jus' figured dat a fair trade wasn't a robbery."

"Well, how 'bout I scrabble yo' brains lose and leave yo' boys to figure out how to put dem shits back together?" Reggie laughed.

"Hold on, Flex. Now I don't think this dis should call fo' any threats of violence or none like dat. You kno' how da game go."

"Maine, I'm gettin' tired of dis nigga," a man in the midst of the crowd said after kissing his teeth.

A flashback quickly popped into the imagine of my head. It wasn't a good one either. It took me back to the day we took over the one way back in Jackson Ward. Flex extracted his pistol from his waist and raised it at eye level. Mack went for his pistol but was a second too slow. Lil' Shawty and Two had both pulled pistols of their own out of their purse. "I wish da fuck you would," Lil' Shawty urged Mack.

Flex weaved through the small crowd of five, approaching the same dude who was just speaking out of turn. "Come here," Flex demanded, grabbing him up by the collar of his shirt. "So you tired, huh?" he asked the man face to face. "You want somebody to put yo' bitch ass to sleep fo' real?" Dude was speechless which was a wise choice.

"Chill, Flex, all dat extra shit ain't even called fo'." Now Mack was trying to reverse his demeanor. "I'll get you da rest of da bread."

"Fuck you, nigga!" Flex spit literally as saliva flew from his mouth. He waved his gun inches away from Mack's face. "And fuck dat money too, pussy. Since y'all broke ass niggas wanna play des broke nigga mind games, how 'bout I make sure all y'all niggas starve out dis bitch? Don't forget I'm da reason y'all niggas even start gettin' money in da first place." It was no secret that Flex's temperament was on fire. The thing that surprised me though was the fact that Flex hadn't killed or at least shot anyone by now.

"Aye, wat d fuck we got goin' on outcha?" About four apartments from where we stood, two men stumbled out of the door stepping off the porch. The first man cradled an ARP in his hands. I felt sorry for him though because the gun was pointed towards the ground. "Why da fuck you got yo' hands on my brother like dat, nigga?" Da second man out the door asked with pistols in both hands. One from the triangular muzzle. I recognized it to be a Desert Eagle. The other was definitely a Glock. Both of the men approached with cautious speed.

Flex cut a quick eye at Lil' Shawty. Obviously he had trained her well. Without Flex even having to utter a word, Lil' Shawty swung her gun towards the approaching invaders and immediately applied the seven pounds of pressure to the trigger, giving the chambered bullets permission to fly toward their targets. Two, being the perfect follower, followed suit. The ARP carrier got shot twice, stumbling back, tripping into a fall; he raised the ARP up releasing shots that touched nothing but clouds.

Mack tried to run, ducking and weaving in a zigzag motion. Flex shot three shots in his direction. A bullet slammed into the back side of Mack's shoulder causing his body to jerk. Two more shots, and his body was meeting the pavement. Flex directed the pistol into dude whom he had in the grasp of his hand. No hesitation involved, Flex dismembered the face of his target blowing up his face with the explosion of the gun. From there he aimed at armed and disarmed targets alike. Letting off rounds like a desperado Mexico warring against the cartel.

Even though they had the ups with the head start, they were outnumbered and outgunned. The only thing that Flex, Lil' Shawty, and Two had against their opposition was the ability to outsmart them. They huddled up amongst each other letting off shots at their opps as they backed their way through the parking lot towards the car. Get da car Two! Flex yelled over the crying pistols. Thank God Flex had left the car running. Two around to the driver's side and hopped behind the wheel. She tapped the horn twice, calling the other two to get their asses in the car. Before we pulled off a demon showed up snatching the soul of the man that Flex had sent to the other side. Only one other person out there was dead and he was snatched by a demon as well. Just like they were gone.

Soon we were gone away from the scene. All was quiet except the continuation of Money Man Epidemic. The song was another lifetime. Lil' Shawty and Flex sat in the back seat and held each other close. Reggie sat in the empty passenger seat beside Two. He called himself flirting and feeling on Two as she drove. He slid his hands in between her thick thighs, felt and squeezed on her titties. She was barely fazed though. With the exception of the cool breezed that rolled up her skin, causing chill bumps to crawl up her arm. She shivered. "Dat shit got my nerves bad," she said. Lil' Mark laughed. I shook my head. Burga looked like he regrets ever coming along with me. But I would get us home. I had too. Even if it cost me.

Chapter Seventeen

Flex

Redemption

Later That Night—

You never know if you have really changed until you are truly tempted. With that being said, either I've never changed or maybe it's just that the demon deep down in you always lays dormant. At a time like this, I was glad that I had that side of me to call on. Fat had received word about what happened. To be honest, I was hoping that it wouldn't cross his table. I really won't trying to hear anything that opposed my will. I definitely didn't want to repeat my mistake of dealing with Fat the same way I did Q. Of course, Fat would hear what went on. At least one side of the story. The population was only hundreds of people in a place where everyone knew Fat. On top of that, they couldn't help but to talk about the new dude that he brung in town, one of his long-lost brothers, me.

Shocked the hell out of me though, Fat was pissed. He was enraged at the way things had gone down. He even apologized to me for allowing me to even deal with Mack. He said Mack was a piece of shit. That he had just come home not too long ago and every time he touched down he stirs up big commotions similar to this. And to think, I thought it was me. Safe to say dude met his match. Well, then again maybe not. Nigga want a match for the Flex master. Fat ran down the game to me about Mack and his gang. Said like most hustlers that they were night owls. He suggested that we waited until then to pull back up on them niggas. I asked him was he even a least bit concerned about us going to shoot up his property. He calmly advised me to let him worry about that. Earlier I had got a call from Mack, this was after the shooting. This nigga talked all types of shit. Screaming and threatening me to pull back up. Where the fuck they do that at? Dude was straight on some twelve shit. He also told me that I shot like a bitch; I laughed at that. But come to find out the two wounds he received were both flesh wounds. Tonight, though, I'd make sure each bullet he caught cracked his cranium.

When Fat had pulled up earlier, he put me onto something else that I hadn't seen coming. In the basement of the family house a temporary expedient closet was built into one of the walls. Fat removed the lock from the double doors and slid them apart. Once they open, an arsenal of weapons were spread across the wall, I couldn't believe this country ass nigga was packing all this steel. Then again, I had to remind myself that this was one of my brothers I was talking about. At this point, I had learned to never be surprised by them for one moment. Fat removed a Russian AK-47 off the wall and threw the strap attached to it over his shoulder. Afterwards, he grabbed for a sawed off 12-gauge pump. Once he told me the Glock .40's had switches on them, I snatched two and extra thirty round clips. Aside from the pistols, I equipped myself with a draco. Lil' Shawty and Two even attempted to grab a couple tools. They reminded me that they were still riding until the wheels fell off. I respected their gangster to the fullest. But because Lil' Shawty carried my seed, so I suggested that they both stay back. I damn near had to beg for them to honor my request. This would actually be the first time since we left the city that we would be splitting up. I understand their feelings but I had to consider the future of us all.

On Fat's request a couple of gunslingers of his had pulled up right before we headed out. Fat enlightened me that they were his personal hitmen. A couple soldiers who've been trained in the military. Never be surprised, I reminded myself. Fat introduced the two men as Lamar and Frank. I doubt if those were their real names. I could care less though, as long as them niggas knew how to kill. Even though I knew it was a struggle for them to do so, Lil' Shawty and Two stayed back with Fat's' wife. The four of us, Fat, Lamar, Frank, and I jumped into my truck and headed towards the mission. Fat reached into a small bag and pulled out a ski mask and handed them to each of us. I was resentful but took it anyway. Hands on the steering wheel, eyes focused on the road, I wondered what and why? What the fuck was I doing and why? More importantly, I wanted to know. "Why you doin' dis, Fat?" I found myself asking him.

"Wat? You gettin' cold feet or some lil' brah?" he asked, not in a teasing manner, yet I still felt slightly disrespected. I been stepping since the Flintstones. Ain't a way for my feet to cold as much as I ran through hell. On some real nigga shit though, and this was just between you and me, I was having mixed feelings. It was like voices in my head. Not the voices of my regular mind, though. It was as if someone was trying to tell me something with a warning. It was just hard for me to pick up on the signal with all the other shit that was on my mind. Q has been on my mind as heavy as ever all day. I wondered if it was him that was trying to reach me. If so, I prayed he speaks louder so I could hear his voice clearly.

But still though, I spoke with a spike of pride to Fat. "Now I ain't got no ma'fuckin' cold feet. Yo' got me fucked up, bra. I'm just sayin' you got all dis shit goin' fo' you in life. Why would you want to throw it all away fo' a nobody like me? I mean you ain't even hesitate to ride. Ain't try to talk me out da shit or none of dat. Instead, you helped me do da wrong thing better."

"First of all, brah, yo' far from nobody. Matter o'fact nigga, you ain't even jus' anybody. You my ma'fuckin' blood. My brother. Pops taught me a lot but two of the main things were family and loyalty. Since I've had knowledge of you and Q, all I've ever dreamed of was havin' a life wit my other halves. Now dat I got you by my side, nigga, I'll risk it all to keep you here. Da fuck I look like bringing you in and den lettin' a nigga try you? Do me a favor and never ask me dumb ass questions like dat ever in yo' life." In the little time that I've known Fat he always remained cool and calm, sometimes even a little too calm. More passive like. I was beginning to take him as a pushover. At this moment though he was anything but that. This nigga was livid. So much so that he wanted to push something over himself. This nigga went from Q to a Flex real quick. "Hold up. Pull ova right here and park." He directed me. "I kno' des niggas posted. Already waitin' fo' us to pull up. As soon as we drive thru dat gate dem niggas gone light dis car up. At least if dey was smart." Fat threw the mask over his face. "Mask up." He looked to me through the two holes on dis almost invisible face in the absent light of night time. I did. "Come on, let's go." Fat led. We followed.

We walked all the way around to the back of the small complex. It was surrounded by a wired fence that separated the apartment from the wilderness of the woods. After stepping through natural brush woods and mazing through trees, we came upon a hole in the fence. At about two feet wide and four feet in length we all had to duck down to make it through the hole. Fat ducked, walked over to a nice size green box. We trailed his movements. "A'ight, look," he said, "we gone trap des niggas from both ends. Two of us goin' right. Da other two left. Da only thing dey gone be able to do is scatter through the parkin' lot. Dats wat we want though. Keep pushin' dem niggas out' til dey ass haul assin' out da entrance gate. Da car already is in a good position. After we handle business, we need to make sure dat all of us make it to dat car simultaneously." Fat took over to the pair of established soldiers. "No man left behind, right?"

"Right," we all agreed

"Bet one more thing, y'all niggas keep ya eyes open. But you should kno' dat already. Especially you, Flex. Y'all niggas da vets. I jus' got da map of da territory. With dat being said, watch out fo' any straggling shooters dat may slide out of one of des apartments. If shit get too ugly before we make it to da other side of da parking lot, don't be too prideful to retreat and leave back out da way we came. If one withdraws, we all do." He looked over at me when he said that last sentence. "Y'all niggas ready?" Fat asked. We said nothing, only confirmed with a nod. "A'ight,' y'all two go left. Flex, you come wit me, let's move out."

No matter how it went down from here, I was proud of Fat, to say the least. Not only did he orchestrate the drill like a true sergeant, but he was also willing to put it all on the line like a true soldier. After making the split, Fat and I paused at the end of the long apartment building. From the great distance of the other end of the building, the soldiers gave it a go by flashing a quick light from one of their fully equipped assault rifles. From the cue, I took the lead, stealthy making my way around the corner. At the edge of the building, I made a quick stop. Taking a peek around the corner, I observed the scene; like Fat said, they were deep. It didn't look like they were ready for war, though. These niggas was shooting dice and taking shots of liquor. This wasn't the type of shoot-out I popped out for. A wave of disrespect washed over me. These niggas don't have a clue who the hell they fucking with. Time to let them know.

I rolled around the corner, waving the Draco in anticipation, taking in the dumb looks on the stupid niggas faces. I let out a growl as I applied the pressure to the trigger of the Draco. Instead, I was the one looking stupid my unexpected hesitation even threw Fat off for a moment. He looked over to me with a look like *what the fuck?* I cocked the Draco and, as expected, one bullet flew out of the chamber. That caught the attention of my prey who paid my ass no mind at first. They looked startled for only a half of a second. It didn't take them long to realize what was going on. Niggas whipped out their pistols and sent a cloud of shots raining down on us from multiple guns. Everything went dark. I became deaf to all sounds. My whole life flashed through my eyes. I suddenly had the feeling of fear. It wrapped around me in a struggling grasp. It was the fear of dying with regret. The fear of not having a chance to right my wrongs. The fear of leaving from my mistakes but not being able to live out the lessons. The fear of understanding.

Amazingly though, grace, the volume of life was being turned back up. *Kat! Kat! Kat! Kat!* I knew that sound from anywhere. That was the sound of an AK-47. I opened my closed eyes and witnessed the uproar amongst me. I knew it's highly doubtful, but have you ever stood underneath a raining cloud without having a drop of the heavenly drip splash onto your skin? I know right. Me neither. In similarity it happened at this very moment. Instead, though, the soft and harmless rain drops were substituted for the hard-shelled damaging bullets. All the shots sent my way missed me, not even coming close. It was complex to my thoughts because the range was so close that even my unborn child could catch a corpse from here. Seeing Fat let off shots of his own reminded me why we were here in the first place. He held it down thus far.

I dropped the Draco to my side in my left hand and used my right to remove the Glock .40 with the switch. Upping the pistol, I aimed high, looking to take a few heads off. "Glock, don't fail me now," I silently whispered a prayer right before I pulled the trigger. Numerous bullets spat out of the gun. The weight of the pistol became heavy as if I couldn't control it with my own strength. It was a very familiar feeling that I remembered feeling before one that I could never forget. Instead of the bullets washing over head and shoulders, they contacted thighs, knees, shins, and feet. Nothing was going right with this ambush. It was some of the weirdest shit that was happening. I almost heard that it was my time to go. Seems that whenever that number was truly called, nothing could prevent that alarm from going off. Even snoozing it. No matter how much ammunition you carried, there was nothing stopping the sand from pouring to the bottom of the hour glass. Not even a single grain.

Chapter Eighteen

Q

Playing in the Rain

The whole ride over here I attempted to scream in Flex's ear. I was trying to get him to change his mind. To turn around and leave the situation as it was. You know that was a difficult task. Not just because I spoke from another world, but because Flex was so damn head strong. There was actually a time where I thought I almost had him. That was until that other brother of ours, Fat, regenerated Flex's ego.

It was super important that I found a way to stop Flex from sliding tonight. Not only was I tired of him killing, but he was literally one kill away from the suffers of hell. How do I know that, right? Well, that's the same thing I asked the source of where the information came from. Not too long before Flex, Fat, and the other two riders hopped into the car, Bitch, Hoe, Pig, and Snake, had paid them a little visit. Their main objective was to make sure that they got deep into Fat's head, using him as the influence to keep Flex from backing out of the idea. At first I thought the demons were there to capture the souls on the loose. They assured us that we was the least concerned. They say that they all were here for Flex. They enlightened us that Flex was going through a time of grace period. That if he failed to make a turnaround within the time the God had appointed him, that he would fall completely in the arms of Satan. From here all it took was one more kill. When I asked them how did they know all of that, they all looked at me as if I was crazy, laughing and going ghost. "I see you at da party, Q," Pig flirted before disappearing completely with the rest.

After hearing the finality of Flex's life here on earth, even Reggie felt the will to repulse from his intended pretensions. "Wat da hell can we possibly do to stop des fools from smokin' each other?" he asked me as we all followed the four steppers through the woods surrounding the apartments.

"I don't know, Reggie," I replied. "Not so long ago you were very determined to find a way of killing him, right? Without knowing how?"

"Yeah but—"

"A'ight then. Use that same determination to try to stop it." The quadripartite hunters split into pairs of two, my soul brothers and I stayed close to Flex and Fat. "It has to be something that we could do," I said, mostly thinking out loud. Flex took the lead and headed around the corner with Fat right on his heels. Flex roared like a lion while he raised the Draco he held in hand. I jumped my apparition body in front of Flex in a failed attempt to get his attention. I'd seen it in his eyes. He was about to go Rambo. For the third time in his lifetime, he had a gun pointed right at my head. I looked down the barrel of the gun and thought fast. Before Flex could pull the trigger with intent to free the bullets from the stick, I tried my hand by sticking a finger in the muzzle.

Flex squeezed with all his might but the bullets weren't released. I looked back at Reggie. Burga laughed. I smiled one of joy.

"It worked," Reggie announced.

"I wonder, wat else can we do?" Lil' Mark asked but was too impatient to wait on an answer. He correspondingly took control of the AK 47 in Fat's hand. By the time Fat was squeezing the trigger, Lil' Mark was directing the rifle in a way that caused the bullets to perfectly outline the bodies of Fat's targets. Lil' Mark laughed in amusement. "Oh shit, check dis shit out," he said, amazed himself. I'm one hundred percent sure that it would be unseeable to the naked eye. But to ours we could see the bullets drawing a dotted line around the figures. It resembles a connect-the-dot sheet.

Reggie slid over to the opposition of my brothers. As they raised their guns, Reggie pushed them all upward. It was like the matrix once he got the concept; Burga fell by his side to give him a pair of hands. A crate full of bullets flew into the wind with no purpose at all. "Des niggas think dey doing some." Reggie laughed in mockery. The faces on all the potential murderers were deadly. The only thing was that they weren't killing anything.

Giving up on the baby AK, Flex dropped it to his side while still holding onto it in his left hand. His next move was to draw the Glock .40 with the thirty shot extended clip hanging from the butt of the gun. His motions were quick. For the safety of his life, he acted in a state of desperation. He pressured the trigger. Just in time I was able to get a hand on top of the pistol, pushing it downward in hopes of it shooting the ground up. Flex had a strong will. He dug more strength from the core of his soul, trying to raise the height of the gun. I couldn't let him do it. I placed both of my hands on the gun, trying to keep it low. Bullets ceaselessly went through me as if I wasn't even there. A few people got touched from the bullets that spat out of Flex's gun. Thankfully, they were all leg shots and I assumed that they would live hopefully.

"Ahh, dis shit easy!" Reggie shouted over the musical gunfire.

"No bullshit," Lil' Mark agreed. "Dis shit fun too, never thought I'll be aiming not hittin' a ma'fucka though!" he confessed. "Watch dis, y'all." Lil' Mark aimed the assault rifle at the feet of one of the men. Barely missing them, the man kicked up his feet repeatedly, high stepping them in place. "Dis nigga out here tap dancing and shit." We all shared a laugh. I had to admit it was hilarious to see that fool acting so silly in the heat of the moment. The dude dropped his gun. It fumbled to the ground; still in a panic, he ran off kicking up more dust with his feet still trying not to step on a bullet. "Stupid niggas," laughed Lil' Mark.

"Wat da fuck are y'all doing?" I sprang higher into the air, startled. Not just from the loud voice screaming in my face. But the additional fact that this bitch had just appeared out of thin air. Looking as sexy as ever. I don't think I could ever get used to that popping up shit though. "Y'all stupid ma'thafuckas fuckin' up our party!" I noticed that Bitch had her three monstrous demons along with her. "I fuckin' hate you, Q. I wish I never would of gave yo' soft ass none of dis good pussy. You bitch ass nigga! Move!" Bitch pushed me away from Flex. The force was heavy. It tossed me to the ground, causing me to roll around in the dirt that laid off to the side of the building. Bitch helped lift Flex's gun higher. Thank God by the time she did, the switch on the gun had permitted all the bullets to sprout out. "Aauuughhh!" Bitch screamed at the top of her lungs.

I lifted my soul back up and flew back towards Bitch. I really wasn't sure what I would do going up against a demon. But it had to be worth a try. I pushed her. It worked, but barely. From there a riot had jumped off between their gang and ours. The fight was mainly over the control of the guns. As mystified and strong as they were, I wasn't sure if we would win this battle against these grim demons. It seemed unlikely.

Chapter Nineteen

Flex

Touched by an Angel

I can't believe I just let off the whole clip of the extension without killing a soul. On top of that shit, the fucking Draco choked up on me. I was looking like a straight clown out here in the middle of a shootout. A real dummy. I thought I died twice within the last minute. Crazy thing was: not only did Fat miss every shot he aimed, but so did the opps. Something wasn't right. I'm not sure what it was but I felt it in my bones. Someone somewhere had to have some type of unseen hands in this warfare.

Fat and I had our back towards the side of the building; we had to fall back in order to reload. Fat had let off the whole fifty rounds from the clip of the K and ain't hit shit. I'm talking about *nothing*. Not even a pinky toe. After all that shit he talked in the car on the way over here. Like he was O-Dogg and I was Kaine. I found out his ass was faking to the max. I couldn't count him out just yet though. Like I said, I think it was some unexplainable shit that was going on beyond the sights of the eye. Just in case I was wrong about the sook's and it was true that Fat really was a scrub, I was more than willing to hold my own. Even his, if that's what I had to do.

I removed the empty clip front the Glock and replaced it with a full one. Fat leaned the AK up against the wall of the building and reversed the 12-gauge strapped to his back around to his front side. "Dis all I got left," he warned me.

I aimed the Draco into the air and pulled the trigger. A single shot echoed, creating a wave of sounds into the air. "Wat da fuck?" I asked, puzzled, bringing the Draco closer to my eyes for examination. "Dis some crazy shit," I mumbled to myself. The gun worked perfectly fine. I handed it over to Fat. "Save dat," I told him, speaking on the pump. "And take dis." I pulled out the twin to my Glock .40. "I got one more extra clip left. We gotta make dis count."

Meanwhile, around the corner, the other half of our little army was showing out on a nigga. They held it down like the real troops they were. "Let's roll out. We gotta pull our weight," I said to Fat. Together we round the corner in another attempt to play grim reaper. A game I had long ago mastered. The first chance he got, Fat silenced my quiet doubt. The draco bullets ripped holes in the backs of a crowd who focused on the other half of our gang. Bodies fell crashing into the others who shot for their lives. That caused them to refocus their attention on Fat and I. Hitting the switch on the glizzy's, I sprayed the bullets like a water hose. That still ain't work. I was starting to feel as if my luck was fucked. Like the devil had finally betrayed his protégé. I don't know why I let that disloyal fucker take me this far. Just for him to drop me off into a pile of shit.

Suddenly a shock of bliss touched my soul. I can't explain exactly where it came from, but I knew it was there something was telling me to get the fuck from around here. Yet my soul and ego was at a tug of war. I did what I thought I'd never do, froze up. Though in actuality it only lasted for a millisecond that would have been enough to lose my life. Within that millisecond of a time, my mind was illustrated with two different outcomes from this next decision I made. The first one everything was all good. Even better than the way things have been going in the last few months. It was as if I had triumph over all my current trials. I saw myself in a true position of monarch that was earned. Not taken. I was loved and respected. Not hated and feared. I even saw my son. I knew it was him. He looked and acted just like Q, though. That part tripped me out. His mother there as well. Still by my side. Amazingly, her and Two. I was super curious as to the road I had to travel to make it to that destination. Then there was the other version of the future. It ended right here, in the next minute or so. All there was to see was a funeral full of crying faces. A graveyard full of confused souls. And then one that was the most unwanted. It was Q and I. We we're together again beefing with each other in hell repeatedly murdering one another just to have to watch the other come right back.

"Retreat, retreat, retreat!" I yelled three times to the top of my lungs. "Fat! Let's get da fuck out'cha here!" I demanded over the shouting bullets. We didn't even halfway complete the mission. There was no way we could make our way through the parking lot. We was forced to head back into the woods. I never was afraid to die. But when knowing you have the chance to live your best life, why would I not choose that life over death? Collectively, we all met up at the hole in the gate. Soon after, we were stepping back through the woods, heading back to the car in haste.

Chapter Twenty

Q

Army of Angels

While Flex and Fat took the time to recuperate, the demons gave a helping hand to Lamar and Frank at killing off a good amount of the enemy. Reggie, Burga, Lil' Mark and I did our best at trying to save some of the lives from both sides. Just couldn't save them all. Just by themselves I assumed that Lamar and Frank could have taken all of the opposite side out with their own skill. If it wasn't for us intervening, I'm pretty certain this battle would have been over. Even without the lacking help of Flex and Fat. The first three bodies fell back-to-back. The angels of death appeared in a very nonchalant state. It was the normality of their jobs. This is what they were created to do. Snatch souls. That's what they did. To my surprise two were good and one bad. The souls released from their bodies look the same as the rest of us when we exit the door of our body, confused. "Wat da fuck!" the bad soul said. Who da fuck are y'all?" he contested. Burga laughed in his face while pushing a gun out of the face of another person.

"Maine, shut yo' soft ass up and help a nigga!" Reggie yelled.

"Help y'all?" the lost soul new to this world said, sucking his teeth and balling his face up. "Fuck I'ma help y'all for? Ion even kno' y'all niggas. Matta fact!" he said, looking down at his soul body. "Wat da fuck is going on? Why da fuck I ain't—" Before he could finish his statement, a demon showed up the way they liked to do and snatched him up. In literally no time he was out of our way. I knew it wouldn't be long before an entourage of demons showed up. "Wat y'all need us to do?" one of the good souls asked, willing to help after hearing the conversation of his late friend.

"First thing," I said while redirecting the aim off another, "do not let the demon wrap their arms around you. If they do, they will take your soul. Other than that, try saving someone or stopping one of these demons."

As I expected, demons were showing up by the twos. "Damn, Bitch!" one of them yelled upon arrival. "Why da fuck is da party so late?"

"Cuz of des bitch ass niggas!" Bitch replied, screaming like a spoiled child at a birthday party who didn't receive her most wanted gift. The demon that just got here took a quick glance at what was going on. After making their observation, they charged towards the soul closest to them. Outnumbered we battled against the demons in combat. While at the same time trying to prevent bullets from hitting the bodies of the humans. Unfortunately, though, two more fell. Their souls were snatched; one good, the other bad. Yet, once they caught an eye of what was going on, they immediately fell in line. For the most part we had to do a lot of bobbing and weaving, trying to remain out of the arms of the demons. I punched a couple of them in the face, using all the strength that I thought I could muster. However, it only pained them a little and pissed them off a lot.

Bitch was the first one to meet Flex and Fat as they exposed themselves from around the corner. She grabbed hold of the Draco in Fat's hand and assisted him in taking down three more bodies. That was three more souls floating in the mist. Two was bad. One got caught slipping. He was gone now. And so was the demon that took him. Flex went to raise both of his pistols. I grabbed and waved the off away from the crowd. Bitch rushed over and tried to remove my hands off the gun. I wouldn't let her. I'd rather let her take me back to her dwelling, where I would wait my turn to burn in hell, before I allowed her to put this last kill on Flex soul. This battle field was getting lopsided by the second as more joined the party. It started to feel enormously difficult to win this one. Or to even come out without losing it all. It was all on the line right now. What we all honestly needed was for Flex to get out of his gangster emotions and put the gun down. Little did he know, he needed it more than all of us.

A quiet storm was starting to accumulate in the sky above our heads. Though I don't think that it was the regular earthly storm. The clouds circled amongst each other in a way I've never seen before. It darkened and created a hole. Through that hole flew an army of angels. Some rode in one of the three chariots that were dragged by these brilliant horses. The horses were pale with satin skin shining like the color of a pearl. They were out fitted in armor rode by angels, who themselves were dressed in armor. Breastplates of iron. Long garments with metal sleeves, silver and gold. Large swords on their sides, fierce helmets on their heads, and they covered their face all but their eyes and mouth. They were formatted in ranks. The last to exit the storm of the cloud was the one I'd seen before. It was the archangel, Michael. He hovered in the sky.

Michael raised a trumpet and blew it. With that, the ladder from the heavens was dropped from the sky. Additional angels climbed down the rungs of the ladders. Next, the archangel tossed a lightning bolt into a cloud. As I've seen before, the cloud accumulated multiple strikes of lighting that struck the presence of the demons. A good number of demons were smoked to ashes. The others were only stunned for a certain phase.

With the large amount of angels that showed up, the battle had now flipped in our favor in a dramatic way. The demons were served drastic punishments. If I was on the wrong side of the war, it wouldn't even have been funny. They didn't stand a chance.

Angels took the new arriving souls to their graves. The defeated demons were reduced to ashes. I could tell from the size and gracefulness of a particular angel that he was another archangel. He approached Flex's side and laid a hand on his forehead. Flex paused for a second in contemplation. That second seemed like a lifetime in his eyes. The archangel flew off. Not even bothering to lend a hand in the war. Once Flex's senses came back to the moment of now, I knew he had gotten the picture. He was calling to the small army of his to fall back and head out. I was overjoyed.

"I'm very disappointed in you, DeQuan," the angel I remembered as ZQ said, as she approached me draped in her heavenly armor. "You disobeyed the laws of Allah." The look on my face was sad. "Yet, you manage to use your will for a very great understandable reason. I shall pray to God for mercy and forgiveness on your soul." Now the angel Mark was coming near. "And you too." ZQ continued looking between Reggie and Lil' Mark. "You both should be very grateful that you were dragged into this task for now, we will finally be able to convey you to your graves." With the help of the angel Mark and a couple of others, Reggie, Lil' Mark, Burga, and I were dropped off at our graves. Reggie was in another cemetery. We said our 'see you laters' in hopes that we shall one day meet up in the heavens someday, God willing.

"I almost doubted you for a while, Q!" Burga said as we chilled on the tombstones of our homely graves.

"You know, Burga?" I asked without wanting an answer. "I thank you for that. I'm not sure how far I would have gone without your doubt." He looked at me funny. "It pushed me to have the confidence in myself that I've been missing."

He cleared his face up. "I'm an alchemist." He laughed.

Chapter Twenty-One

Flex All Falls Down

One Month Later

At the family's house I sat on the porch with Lil' Shawty, Two, Fat, his wife and son, and Slim and the dogs. Blowing the smoke of Fat's famous countryside wed, I thought back on the success of the last month. Most of my numbers had tripled. It was like ever since I decided to change my life in the middle of a shootout, my whole life changed for the better. I felt bigger than a boss. I finally felt like a king. A real king. The king I always wanted to be. With a kingdom, empire, and even a queen. Everything a king could ever ask for. There was only one more problem I had to face.

I saw them through the cloud of smoke that hung in the air in front of my face. The tires of their cars kicking up dust of their own speeding on the gravel. The dogs being hipped, just as soon as I was flying off the porch in the pursuit to protect our land from its intruders. "Wat da fuck?" Fat wondered.

"Lil' Shawty, Two," I said, breaking them out of their laughter. "Y'all goin da house." Immediately they stopped laughing. "Dey here," I announced. I had gone over these circumstances with them a few times. I was tired of running and knew it would come a time to face my past. The more I tried to run away from it, the longer I would prolong living the life I really wished to leave.

"You need us to scrap up, Flex?" Fat questioned anxious.

"Naw, we good, brah, jus' chill." Lil' Shawty gave me the kiss of a lifetime, followed by Two. They both showed me how much they loved me and assured me they would be there every step of the way. "I love y'all too." Afterwards they did as we promised the plan would go.

"So who da fuck is dat?" Fat dug deeper into his suspicion.

"It's 12," I simply said. They pulled up and hopped out the cars as if they were expecting a major shoot-out or something. Calmly I stood with my hands in the air and stepped off the property.

An officer on the front line cocked his shotgun and aimed it in the direction of my head. "Don't make another fucking move!" I froze. The dogs were going crazy. Viciously barking at the legs of the law.

"Vick! Honey!" Fat called out to them all by using the two main names. "Y'all get y'all asses ova here! Now! All y'all." I could tell they were reluctant to do so. But they listened to the man who trained and cared for them.

"Get da fuck on the ground! Now!" the leading detective from Richmond homicide said through the bullhorn on his car. It was Graham. This shit wasn't funny but I smiled. I smiled because he still had no idea that his daughter was with me. Right behind the doors of that house. Lil' Shawty and Two had gotten fake IDs, socials and the whole nine. They would change their identities to symbolically kill their old selves to make their future movements smooth. They had a good life here. I was more than sure that they would only grow. Even after I'm locked away and gone. Starting with one knee, hands still up. I made my way to the ground. A pair of officers had rushed me. They yanked my hands behind my back and cuffing them. Then I heard the statement I always hated hearing the most. "Deshawn Anderson, you are under arrest—anything you say can and will be used against you—you have the right to—" Y'all know how that shit go. I blocked it out and dreaded the ride back to Richmond.

Four Weeks Later—

You know they weren't giving a nigga like me a bond. I still tried my hand twice though just to waste their time and money. I decided to decline the right to counsel and represented myself. I ain't want none of them crooked ass lawyers by my side faking. I ain't give a fuck if they were black or white. In my eyes they all had the same motive and took the same oaths. Besides, you know my brother and my baby momma got a bag. They were searching for the best lawyer that money could buy. It took them so long because I told them to take their time. I wanted someone that wasn't from this state. That way, at least, I knew they wouldn't owe any favors from the past. Trying to sell a nigga out like a slave at an auction.

Today was the preliminary hearing of my trial. Most of the charges were trumped up. Like trying to throw the RICO at me without me even having a gang to commit organized crimes with. Tried to hit me with the ring leader. Of what circus though? Shit I was exiled, banished. They even reached as far as talking kingpin talk. They definitely had the wrong nigga on that shit. The witness tampering sounded accurate. I just couldn't think of who. It was just a whole bunch of assumptions. Some were true. Like murder in the first degree. That sounds more about right. I was really unsure if they had any actual evidence. We'll see. But I ain't gone say too much else about that right now. People probably watching and listening right now. One thing I was certain to be fucked on was probation. "So, Mr. Anderson, I take it that you are moving forward with representing yourself?" The judge assumed.

"Yo' Honor, I really feel like it would be best if I—"

"Your Honor, excuse me." A person had badged through the doors of the courtroom, cutting me off at mid-sentence.

"But I will be representing Mr. Anderson from here on out if there's no problems with the court." I looked behind towards the direction of the voice. She was even more beautiful as ever. I felt blessed to be saved. Instead of Satan sending demons at me in an attempt to cause corruption, God now sent me angels to make peace.

"No, Ms. Morning. I don't see why the courts would have a problem," the judge assured. "If anything, you should be asking Mr. Anderson. He's pretty confident that he'll—"

"I'll accept her representation yo' honor." I agreed.

After the court arrangement was over my lawyer called me in for a visit. We sat face to face in a confined room. "Why did you come to help me?"

"I'm here on behalf of yo' brother. This wat he would have wanted me to do. Besides, it's wat family does. He helped me get to where I am now. Since he's not here in order for me to pay him back, I decided that you would be in need of legal assistance."

"So you sayin' I'm just a charity case?" I asked sarcastically.

"No, I'm sayin' dat dis is how family is supposed to treat each other. Not kick each other when we're down. Pull them down, they are up. Or keep them stagnant when they are lookin' fo' change."

"Okay, okay, I get you. Don't rub it in. You not afraid dat dis could be a conflict of interest."

"You don't have to be blood to be family. And ders really no trace of Q and our relations except our son. But as long as you follow my lead and let me—"

"Hold up." I had to cut her off. "You got a son with my brother?" I came to a halt.

"Yes, he's a Jr and he's comin' upon his first birthday soon."

"Damn." I sat back in the seat and thought of all the surprises of life. "I never got yo' name by da way," I reminded her respectfully.

"Mr. Anderson, my name is Dawn," she uttered. "Dawn Mornings. But you should jus' call me Ms. Mornings for da sake of da case."

"Ms. Mornings," I spoke, having the utmost respect for a woman I once wanted to kill due to ill minded thoughts." I want to apologize and thank you so much—"

"Apology accepted," she cut me off. "But save da thanks 'til after trial, or a bargain for the sweetest plea possible." I smiled. Even without being here Q played a helping hand in my crazy game of life.

Self Made Tay

Chapter Twenty-Two

Q's Reincarnation

We were all chilling in the field of the cemetery. Something. Nothing new except the souls that just came. All of a sudden, the ground shocked and the sky opened. Certain souls were slowly being sucked up into the opening of the sky. Immediately I realized that they were all good souls. Satan went up. Streets followed, then a few others. "That's the call for heaven," Burga enlightened me. Qua went up with Jo Jo and Jowan.

"How come we not going? At least you?" I asked Burga.

"I don't know, Q. Maybe we got to catch the next trip or maybe we messed up by leaving the graveyard in the first place." I looked away from Burga and focused back towards the souls going up. I felt bad. Not for me, though. If you had asked, was it all worth it? I'd say yes. Not only did I get to save my brother from a ticket to hell. I also helped a couple of soul brothers along the way. The only regret I may have was: getting Burga involved into the mix. I looked over to help in preparation to give him some words of encouragement. Astonishingly, I turned only to find Burga's soul floating to the heavens with the rest. He looked as happy as I've ever seen him. Yet it was bitter-sweet. "Keep your head up, Q," he said, approaching the clouds. "And stay out of trouble, I'll see you again. I love you, brah."

"I love you too, brah. Go rest peacefully," I replied happily because my friends were happy. That was real love.

Soon they all started to scream down from the sky. "We love you, Q! Don't worry, brah. We got you!" they said in unison.

"Yeah, when I meet God I'ma ask can he look out for you, Burga said. "And stay sucker free," he added. "You gone be alright. Hold it down for us." Then they were all gone and the sky was closed up as it normally would be.

I released a light sigh. What a life this was to live? I wasn't depressed about being alone. I've been in way worst conditions. I wasn't anxious about what would happen to me in the future. For I knew two things about the future: one was that the future was now, and two, it was destined. I definitely had no regrets about my past. When it came to the dash between my birth and death date on my tombstone at least I can say I gave it all I had. And that was enough for me.

Coming from out of nowhere, an angel approached me from my blindside. It was the angel, Mark. "Hey, DeQuan. I was sent to offer you a merciful missionary from our Lord."

"A what?" I wondered, completely lost.

"You are being handed the option to return back to earth. As the same soul through a different embodiment. The rewards are a chance to be exalted in the graceful eye of our God. Along with exceeding the accumulations of good deeds. And the chance to save plenty others from the pains of terrible lives. Though there are some risks, you will have to be a strong-willed soul for this experience. Otherwise, you could subject yourself to the deaths of hell if you don't remain focused. That's why you were chosen."

"What would I have to do?" I asked.

"Do you accept the offer?" Was all Mark wanted to know.

I thought about it for a dead second, before asking myself what did I have to lose? Life was hard on earth indeed. But after being here I realized that it wasn't much different. Besides, I was always up for a challenge. So I bravely said, "Yes."

Mark took me up to a place in the universe called The Pre-incarnation World. Here the new and returned souls would get a pre-vision of their next lives. Who they would be. What their purpose for being there were. Everything that we searched for while on earth. I realized that all we searched for already knew. It was already in us. We just looked everywhere in the world except there. The next life of mine was definitely a laborious one. All of ours were we all played a big part in the small scheme of things. I was super happy about who I was about to become. The greatness I was about to achieve. The people I was about to meet. And definitely the family I was about to be a part of. There's no way I'd be able to sum it all up so you'll have to catch me in my next lifetime. My last life had nothing on the future me.

Before I did, Mark told me that all I knew would slowly be forgotten as I aged in childhood. But if I believed deep enough and trusted in God and my inner knowledge, that it was a way to suffice it all. "Blessings, DeQuan," he said. I hopped into the fetus of my new mother's womb to begin the journey of a new life.

Self Made Tay

Chapter Twenty-Three

Flex's Intuition

I was finally called out to my first personal visitation. This would be the best visitation I would ever set my eyes on. Almost a month ago my son was born. Of course, he was named after me—Lil' Flex for short. I had pictures and what not. But there would be nothing like us looking into each other's eyes searching for the souls we were with. I walked with confident pride over to the visiting station. Even though I didn't have to go far. I picked up the receiver to activate the screen to start the visit. The first person I saw was Fat. "Yo' ugly ass," I joked, sounding serious but really happy to see him.

"I kno' you ain't talkin'. Nigga you look jus' like me." He laughed in reply.

"Shidd, nigga. I ain't ugly."

"Shidd, me neither nigga. Pops don't make no ugly kids." We both laughed. "Naw, fo' real though, brah. Look who I brought wit me?" Fat moved to the side and allowed Lil' Shawty to come into the screen. She held Lil' Flex in her arms bundled up. She held him up to the screen so we could both see each other. Both his and my eyes lit up like blessed kids on a Christmas morning. Lil' Flex started laughing hilariously as if he was at a Kevin Hart show or something. Fat laughed along with him. "I'm tellin' you, brah. Ion kno' wat it is, but dis a happy as baby. My nephew be geeked up wit his goofy ass. I ain't gone lie though, I ain't never seen him dis hyped."

Though I was in a complete state of serenity, I stared in the face of my son sternly. I wondered how on earth could this be possible? "Wats wrong, boo?" Lil 'Shawty asked. "Why you lookin' at him like dat?" She wanted to know.

"Huh?" Slightly snapped out of my trance but still kept my focus locked in with Lil' Flex. "Naw it's jus' dat—he looks jus' like—Q."

Lil' Flex erupted from my observation which made the assumption that I had even more weird. Lil' Shawty's and Fat's faces were perplexed. Even Two uttered. "Waatt?" From the background of the screen.

"Well, I mean." Lil' Shawty finally spoke. "Y'all all sort of kinda look alike. Y'all genes strong as hell."

"No, I kno' dat. But he looks exactly like Q. Eyes and all." I know they didn't understand. Because to my understanding they pretty much never saw Q. "I talkin' baby pics and all, my son looks like my brother. It's not a bad thing though. Y'all lighten up. It's jus' dat I thought that I'd never see my brother again. But my son has borrowed the face of my brother. Lil' Flex way better looking dan Q was, though. He gets dat from me, of course." I said this to lighten the mode and send everyone into the state of laughter. If they thought I made that comment to be funny, there really wasn't too much of a difference. But was this really happening? Could this even be possible? Was Q really living through my son? Looking through his eyes my son's orbs was identical to the soul of my late brother's. I no longer doubted it. Call me insane or whatever the fuck you want to. I don't give a fuck. But I knew that Lil' Flex has been here before. I knew that he was really Q in the flesh. A smile spread across my face. Q was a real warrior. He was the only man I knew that refused to let death defeat him. He was back again.

"We got one more surprise fo' you too, though," Fat warned me. It was Dawn. she held a big baby in her arms covered in baby designer. "Dis our nephew, brah, Baby Q!" Fat announced. How ironic? I thought to myself. Q's Jr. looking just like our pops and my Jr looking just like Q. these niggas thought they had all the sense from the heavens. But I was hip to them.

"Say hi to yo' uncle, baby Q," Dawn said handing her son off to Fat. "Let me see him?" She reached for Lil' Flex. "Oh my God!" she expressed excitedly. "He looks jus' like Q!" Fat and Lil' Shawty looked at me in the screen. "Dis is crazy." He looks more like Q than his own son. Oh now, I'm takin' him home wit me and my son. Him so handsome. Look at him. "You ever seen a grown woman blush?"

"I told y'all," was all I could say. What more could I say?

-It's Never The End-

Lock Down Publications and Ca$h Presents assisted publishing packages.

BASIC PACKAGE $499
Editing
Cover Design
Formatting

UPGRADED PACKAGE $800
Typing
Editing
Cover Design
Formatting

ADVANCE PACKAGE $1,200
Typing
Editing
Cover Design
Formatting
Copyright registration
Proofreading
Upload book to Amazon

LDP SUPREME PACKAGE $1,500
Typing
Editing
Cover Design
Formatting
Copyright registration
Proofreading
Set up Amazon account
Upload book to Amazon

Advertise on LDP Amazon and Facebook page

***Other services available upon request. Additional charges may apply
Lock Down Publications
P.O. Box 944
Stockbridge, GA 30281-9998
Phone # 470 303-9761

Submission Guideline

Submit the first three chapters of your completed manuscript to ldpsubmissions@gmail.com, subject line: Your book's title. The manuscript must be in a .doc file and sent as an attachment. Document should be in Times New Roman, double spaced and in size 12 font. Also, provide your synopsis and full contact information. If sending multiple submissions, they must each be in a separate email.

Have a story but no way to send it electronically? You can still submit to LDP/Ca$h Presents. Send in the first three chapters, written or typed, of your completed manuscript to:

LDP: Submissions Dept
Po Box 944
Stockbridge, Ga 30281

DO NOT send original manuscript. Must be a duplicate.

Provide your synopsis and a cover letter containing your full contact information.

Thanks for considering LDP and Ca$h Presents.

<u>NEW RELEASES</u>

SOSA GANG 2 by ROMELL TUKES

KINGZ OF THE GAME 7 by PLAYA RAY

SKI MASK MONEY 2 by RENTA

BORN IN THE GRAVE 3 by SELF MADE TAY

BLOOD OF A BOSS **VI**

SHADOWS OF THE GAME II

TRAP BASTARD II

By **Askari**

LOYAL TO THE GAME **IV**

By **T.J. & Jelissa**

TRUE SAVAGE **VIII**

MIDNIGHT CARTEL IV

DOPE BOY MAGIC IV

CITY OF KINGZ III

NIGHTMARE ON SILENT AVE II

THE PLUG OF LIL MEXICO II

CLASSIC CITY II

By **Chris Green**

BLAST FOR ME **III**

A SAVAGE DOPEBOY III

CUTTHROAT MAFIA III

DUFFLE BAG CARTEL VII

HEARTLESS GOON VI

By **Ghost**

A HUSTLER'S DECEIT III

KILL ZONE II

BAE BELONGS TO ME III

TIL DEATH II

By **Aryanna**

KING OF THE TRAP III

By **T.J. Edwards**

GORILLAZ IN THE BAY V

3X KRAZY III

STRAIGHT BEAST MODE III

De'Kari

KINGPIN KILLAZ IV

STREET KINGS III

PAID IN BLOOD III

CARTEL KILLAZ IV

DOPE GODS III

Hood Rich

SINS OF A HUSTLA II

ASAD

YAYO V

Bred In The Game 2

S. Allen

THE STREETS WILL TALK II

By Yolanda Moore

SON OF A DOPE FIEND III

HEAVEN GOT A GHETTO III

SKI MASK MONEY III

By Renta

LOYALTY AIN'T PROMISED III

By Keith Williams

I'M NOTHING WITHOUT HIS LOVE II

SINS OF A THUG II

TO THE THUG I LOVED BEFORE II

IN A HUSTLER I TRUST II

By Monet Dragun

QUIET MONEY IV

EXTENDED CLIP III

THUG LIFE IV

By **Trai'Quan**

THE STREETS MADE ME IV

By **Larry D. Wright**

IF YOU CROSS ME ONCE III

ANGEL V

By **Anthony Fields**

THE STREETS WILL NEVER CLOSE IV

By K'ajji

HARD AND RUTHLESS III

KILLA KOUNTY IV

By Khufu

MONEY GAME III

By Smoove Dolla

JACK BOYS VS DOPE BOYS IV

A GANGSTA'S QUR'AN V

COKE GIRLZ II

COKE BOYS II

LIFE OF A SAVAGE V

CHI'RAQ GANGSTAS V

SOSA GANG III

BRONX SAVAGES II

BODYMORE KINGPINS II

By Romell Tukes

MURDA WAS THE CASE III

Elijah R. Freeman

AN UNFORESEEN LOVE IV

BABY, I'M WINTERTIME COLD III

By **Meesha**

QUEEN OF THE ZOO III

By **Black Migo**

CONFESSIONS OF A JACKBOY III

By Nicholas Lock

KING KILLA II

By Vincent "Vitto" Holloway

BETRAYAL OF A THUG III

By Fre\$h

THE MURDER QUEENS III

By Michael Gallon

THE BIRTH OF A GANGSTER III

By Delmont Player

TREAL LOVE II

By Le'Monica Jackson

FOR THE LOVE OF BLOOD III

By Jamel Mitchell

RAN OFF ON DA PLUG II

By Paper Boi Rari

HOOD CONSIGLIERE III

By Keese

PRETTY GIRLS DO NASTY THINGS II

By Nicole Goosby

PROTÉGÉ OF A LEGEND III

LOVE IN THE TRENCHES II

By Corey Robinson

IT'S JUST ME AND YOU II

By Ah'Million

FOREVER GANGSTA III

By Adrian Dulan

GORILLAZ IN THE TRENCHES II

By SayNoMore

THE COCAINE PRINCESS VIII

By King Rio

CRIME BOSS II

Playa Ray

LOYALTY IS EVERYTHING III

Molotti

HERE TODAY GONE TOMORROW II

By Fly Rock

REAL G'S MOVE IN SILENCE II

By Von Diesel

GRIMEY WAYS IV

By Ray Vinci

<u>Available Now</u>

RESTRAINING ORDER **I & II**
By **CA$H & Coffee**
LOVE KNOWS NO BOUNDARIES **I II & III**
By **Coffee**
RAISED AS A GOON I, II, III & IV
BRED BY THE SLUMS I, II, III
BLAST FOR ME I & II
ROTTEN TO THE CORE I II III
A BRONX TALE I, II, III
DUFFLE BAG CARTEL I II III IV V VI
HEARTLESS GOON I II III IV V
A SAVAGE DOPEBOY I II
DRUG LORDS I II III
CUTTHROAT MAFIA I II
KING OF THE TRENCHES
By **Ghost**
LAY IT DOWN **I & II**
LAST OF A DYING BREED I II
BLOOD STAINS OF A SHOTTA I & II III
By **Jamaica**
LOYAL TO THE GAME I II III
LIFE OF SIN I, II III
By **TJ & Jelissa**
BLOODY COMMAS I & II

SKI MASK CARTEL I II & III

KING OF NEW YORK I II,III IV V

RISE TO POWER I II III

COKE KINGS I II III IV V

BORN HEARTLESS I II III IV

KING OF THE TRAP I II

By **T.J. Edwards**

IF LOVING HIM IS WRONG…I & II

LOVE ME EVEN WHEN IT HURTS I II III

By **Jelissa**

WHEN THE STREETS CLAP BACK I & II III

THE HEART OF A SAVAGE I II III IV

MONEY MAFIA I II

LOYAL TO THE SOIL I II III

By **Jibril Williams**

A DISTINGUISHED THUG STOLE MY HEART I II & III

LOVE SHOULDN'T HURT I II III IV

RENEGADE BOYS I II III IV

PAID IN KARMA I II III

SAVAGE STORMS I II III

AN UNFORESEEN LOVE I II III

BABY, I'M WINTERTIME COLD I II

By **Meesha**

A GANGSTER'S CODE I &, II III

A GANGSTER'S SYN I II III

THE SAVAGE LIFE I II III

CHAINED TO THE STREETS I II III

BLOOD ON THE MONEY I II III

A GANGSTA'S PAIN I II III

By J-Blunt

PUSH IT TO THE LIMIT

By **Bre' Hayes**

BLOOD OF A BOSS **I, II, III, IV, V**

SHADOWS OF THE GAME

TRAP BASTARD

By **Askari**

THE STREETS BLEED MURDER **I, II & III**

THE HEART OF A GANGSTA I II& III

By **Jerry Jackson**

CUM FOR ME I II III IV V VI VII VIII

An **LDP Erotica Collaboration**

BRIDE OF A HUSTLA **I II & II**

THE FETTI GIRLS **I, II& III**

CORRUPTED BY A GANGSTA I, II III, IV

BLINDED BY HIS LOVE

THE PRICE YOU PAY FOR LOVE I, II ,III

DOPE GIRL MAGIC I II III

By **Destiny Skai**

WHEN A GOOD GIRL GOES BAD

By **Adrienne**

THE COST OF LOYALTY I II III

By Kweli

A GANGSTER'S REVENGE **I II III & IV**

THE BOSS MAN'S DAUGHTERS I II III IV V

A SAVAGE LOVE **I & II**

BAE BELONGS TO ME I II

A HUSTLER'S DECEIT I, II, III

WHAT BAD BITCHES DO I, II, III

SOUL OF A MONSTER I II III

KILL ZONE

A DOPE BOY'S QUEEN I II III

TIL DEATH

By **Aryanna**

A KINGPIN'S AMBITON

A KINGPIN'S AMBITION **II**

I MURDER FOR THE DOUGH

By **Ambitious**

TRUE SAVAGE I II III IV V VI VII

DOPE BOY MAGIC I, II, III

MIDNIGHT CARTEL I II III

CITY OF KINGZ I II

NIGHTMARE ON SILENT AVE

THE PLUG OF LIL MEXICO II

CLASSIC CITY

By **Chris Green**

A DOPEBOY'S PRAYER

By **Eddie "Wolf" Lee**

THE KING CARTEL **I, II & III**

By **Frank Gresham**

THESE NIGGAS AIN'T LOYAL **I, II & III**

By **Nikki Tee**

GANGSTA SHYT **I II &III**

By **CATO**

THE ULTIMATE BETRAYAL

By **Phoenix**

BOSS'N UP **I , II & III**

By **Royal Nicole**

I LOVE YOU TO DEATH

By **Destiny J**

I RIDE FOR MY HITTA

I STILL RIDE FOR MY HITTA

By **Misty Holt**

LOVE & CHASIN' PAPER

By **Qay Crockett**

TO DIE IN VAIN

SINS OF A HUSTLA

By **ASAD**

BROOKLYN HUSTLAZ

By **Boogsy Morina**

BROOKLYN ON LOCK I & II

By **Sonovia**

GANGSTA CITY

By **Teddy Duke**

A DRUG KING AND HIS DIAMOND I & II III

A DOPEMAN'S RICHES

HER MAN, MINE'S TOO I, II

CASH MONEY HO'S

THE WIFEY I USED TO BE I II

PRETTY GIRLS DO NASTY THINGS

By Nicole Goosby

TRAPHOUSE KING **I II & III**

KINGPIN KILLAZ I II III

STREET KINGS I II

PAID IN BLOOD **I II**

CARTEL KILLAZ I II III

DOPE GODS I II

By **Hood Rich**

LIPSTICK KILLAH **I, II, III**

CRIME OF PASSION I II & III

FRIEND OR FOE I II III

By **Mimi**

STEADY MOBBN' **I, II, III**

THE STREETS STAINED MY SOUL I II III

By **Marcellus Allen**

WHO SHOT YA **I, II, III**

SON OF A DOPE FIEND I II

HEAVEN GOT A GHETTO I II

SKI MASK MONEY I II

Renta

GORILLAZ IN THE BAY **I II III IV**

TEARS OF A GANGSTA I II

3X KRAZY I II

STRAIGHT BEAST MODE I II

DE'KARI

TRIGGADALE I II III

MURDAROBER WAS THE CASE I II

Elijah R. Freeman

GOD BLESS THE TRAPPERS I, II, III

THESE SCANDALOUS STREETS I, II, III

FEAR MY GANGSTA I, II, III IV, V

THESE STREETS DON'T LOVE NOBODY I, II

BURY ME A G I, II, III, IV, V

A GANGSTA'S EMPIRE I, II, III, IV

THE DOPEMAN'S BODYGAURD I II

THE REALEST KILLAZ I II III

THE LAST OF THE OGS I II III

Tranay Adams

THE STREETS ARE CALLING

Duquie Wilson

MARRIED TO A BOSS I II III

By Destiny Skai & Chris Green

KINGZ OF THE GAME I II III IV V VI VII

CRIME BOSS

Playa Ray

SLAUGHTER GANG I II III

RUTHLESS HEART I II III

By Willie Slaughter

FUK SHYT

By Blakk Diamond

DON'T F#CK WITH MY HEART I II

By Linnea

ADDICTED TO THE DRAMA I II III

IN THE ARM OF HIS BOSS II

By Jamila

YAYO I II III IV

A SHOOTER'S AMBITION I II

BRED IN THE GAME

By S. Allen

TRAP GOD I II III

RICH $AVAGE I II III

MONEY IN THE GRAVE I II III

By Martell Troublesome Bolden

FOREVER GANGSTA I II

GLOCKS ON SATIN SHEETS I II

By Adrian Dulan

TOE TAGZ I II III IV

LEVELS TO THIS SHYT I II

IT'S JUST ME AND YOU

By Ah'Million

KINGPIN DREAMS I II III

RAN OFF ON DA PLUG

By Paper Boi Rari

CONFESSIONS OF A GANGSTA I II III IV

CONFESSIONS OF A JACKBOY I II

By Nicholas Lock

I'M NOTHING WITHOUT HIS LOVE

SINS OF A THUG

TO THE THUG I LOVED BEFORE

A GANGSTA SAVED XMAS

IN A HUSTLER I TRUST
By Monet Dragun
CAUGHT UP IN THE LIFE I II III
THE STREETS NEVER LET GO I II III
By Robert Baptiste
NEW TO THE GAME I II III
MONEY, MURDER & MEMORIES I II III
By **Malik D. Rice**
LIFE OF A SAVAGE I II III IV
A GANGSTA'S QUR'AN I II III IV
MURDA SEASON I II III
GANGLAND CARTEL I II III
CHI'RAQ GANGSTAS I II III IV
KILLERS ON ELM STREET I II III
JACK BOYZ N DA BRONX I II III
A DOPEBOY'S DREAM I II III
JACK BOYS VS DOPE BOYS I II III
COKE GIRLZ
COKE BOYS
SOSA GANG I II
BRONX SAVAGES
BODYMORE KINGPINS
By Romell Tukes
LOYALTY AIN'T PROMISED I II
By Keith Williams
QUIET MONEY I II III
THUG LIFE I II III

EXTENDED CLIP I II

A GANGSTA'S PARADISE

By **Trai'Quan**

THE STREETS MADE ME I II III

By **Larry D. Wright**

THE ULTIMATE SACRIFICE I, II, III, IV, V, VI

KHADIFI

IF YOU CROSS ME ONCE I II

ANGEL I II III IV

IN THE BLINK OF AN EYE

By **Anthony Fields**

THE LIFE OF A HOOD STAR

By Ca$h & Rashia Wilson

THE STREETS WILL NEVER CLOSE I II III

By K'ajji

CREAM I II III

THE STREETS WILL TALK

By Yolanda Moore

NIGHTMARES OF A HUSTLA I II III

By King Dream

CONCRETE KILLA I II III

VICIOUS LOYALTY I II III

By Kingpen

HARD AND RUTHLESS I II

MOB TOWN 251

THE BILLIONAIRE BENTLEYS I II III

REAL G'S MOVE IN SILENCE

By Von Diesel

GHOST MOB

Stilloan Robinson

MOB TIES I II III IV V VI

SOUL OF A HUSTLER, HEART OF A KILLER I II

GORILLAZ IN THE TRENCHES

By SayNoMore

BODYMORE MURDERLAND I II III

THE BIRTH OF A GANGSTER I II

By Delmont Player

FOR THE LOVE OF A BOSS

By C. D. Blue

MOBBED UP I II III IV

THE BRICK MAN I II III IV V

THE COCAINE PRINCESS I II III IV V VI VII

By King Rio

KILLA KOUNTY I II III IV

By Khufu

MONEY GAME I II

By Smoove Dolla

A GANGSTA'S KARMA I II III

By FLAME

KING OF THE TRENCHES I II III

by **GHOST & TRANAY ADAMS**

QUEEN OF THE ZOO I II

By **Black Migo**

GRIMEY WAYS I II III

Self Made Tay

By Ray Vinci
XMAS WITH AN ATL SHOOTER
By Ca$h & Destiny Skai
KING KILLA
By Vincent "Vitto" Holloway
BETRAYAL OF A THUG I II
By Fre$h
THE MURDER QUEENS I II
By Michael Gallon
TREAL LOVE
By Le'Monica Jackson
FOR THE LOVE OF BLOOD I II
By Jamel Mitchell
HOOD CONSIGLIERE I II
By Keese
PROTÉGÉ OF A LEGEND I II
LOVE IN THE TRENCHES
By Corey Robinson
BORN IN THE GRAVE I II III
By Self Made Tay
MOAN IN MY MOUTH
By XTASY
TORN BETWEEN A GANGSTER AND A GENTLEMAN
By J-BLUNT & Miss Kim
LOYALTY IS EVERYTHING I II
Molotti
HERE TODAY GONE TOMORROW

By Fly Rock

PILLOW PRINCESS

By S. Hawkins

<u>BOOKS BY LDP'S CEO, CA$H</u>

TRUST IN NO MAN

TRUST IN NO MAN 2

TRUST IN NO MAN 3

BONDED BY BLOOD

SHORTY GOT A THUG

THUGS CRY

THUGS CRY 2

THUGS CRY 3

TRUST NO BITCH

TRUST NO BITCH 2

TRUST NO BITCH 3

TIL MY CASKET DROPS

RESTRAINING ORDER

RESTRAINING ORDER 2

IN LOVE WITH A CONVICT

LIFE OF A HOOD STAR

XMAS WITH AN ATL SHOOTER

Born in the Grave 3

www.ingramcontent.com/pod-product-compliance
Lightning Source LLC
Chambersburg PA
CBHW071201260626
47162CB00003B/1132